The Diary

J. SINCLAIR WATTS

To Joan,
Happy reading!
J. Sinclair Watts

This book is a work of fiction. Any reference to historical events or real people or real locations is also fiction. Other names, locations, characters, and events are products of the author's imagination, and any resemblance to actual events, locations or people is completely coincidental.

To Pat
Sean, Maya and Rook
Paul, Kim and Kallan

The Diary

A CHARLESTON CHASE MYSTERY

Prologue

ollege of Charleston student Craig Duncan walked down George Street toward the dark archway of Porter's Lodge, angry he'd goofed off so long at the library. Here it was 11 o'clock and he'd missed dinner again. He read the inscription over the arch—"Know Thyself"—as he entered the tunnel-like structure onto the cistern lawn.

"I know myself all right. Always late," he mumbled, his voice echoing in the passage as he shifted his backpack to the other shoulder. He looked up to see a fingernail sliver of moon hovering over the ancient moss-draped oaks.

Unease crept up the nape of his neck as he glanced to his right toward St. Philip Street. He'd had a gut feeling of being watched for a couple of days. And with good reason...he should never have asked for the money. It seemed simple at the time, and he needed the cash if he wanted to come back next semester.

It was just a tiny thing he'd found, romantic. But it

seemed valuable to the construction guy. *I'll give it to him after my exam tomorrow morning.*

He looked again, but no one was there. He scanned the path he'd just walked, muttered "Whatever," to himself and took two steps onto the grassy cistern lawn. He looked again beyond the wrought iron fence to the well-lighted street where a car sloshed by on the asphalt still shiny from the shower earlier in the evening, wishing he'd stayed on the sidewalk instead of taking the shortcut to the dorms. He walked on across the dark yard, the scant light dissolving into watery shadows creeping across the lawn. Pizza smells drifted on the damp night air from D'Allesandro's just down the street. His stomach growled.

He was just here on Friday night with Emily after the Bobby Caldwell concert. His sweet girl. He smiled at the memory. He'd call her when he got back to the dorm…maybe even tap on her window to let him in for the night. The campus cops caught him in the act of sneaking in once last semester—and they banned him from being near her dorm for a month. He'd be more careful tonight. Besides he couldn't wait to show her what he had, then he'd give it to the man tomorrow morning. Hey, it was only a day late. What difference could that make? He was still hoping to get a chunk of money for it.

"Damn," he stumbled on the uneven flagstones embedded in the grass and gave a little hop and almost recovered his stride before falling forward and slamming into what felt like a wall. He clutched air, then grabbed a handful of shirt stretched tight over a massive torso. He patted the chest of whomever had broken his fall.

"Thanks," he said. He looked up to see a dark, large brimmed hat. Who the hell wears a big hat at night in this heat—the fleeting thought sliced through Craig's mind.

He stepped back and made a move to pass by.

"Have a good night," Craig said. The man grabbed the strap of the backpack and pulled it nearly off Craig's shoulder.

"Hey...cut it out," Craig shouted, jerking away, not wanting to lose the find. He couldn't afford for some halfwit mugger to steal what could amount to his future.

He started to run.

Fast.

He took a couple of steps. Home was just ahead.

He'd see Emily...show her what he'd found—it was right up her alley—before giving it up.

He shifted his backpack higher on his shoulder, as he ran, thinking, hoping the man had given up.

He glanced back.

It was the last thing Craig Duncan ever did.

Chapter 1

*J*ack Chase sat on the last of the winged steps leading to the portico of Randolph Hall as he eyed the ordered chaos of the murder scene before him. The College of Charleston campus hadn't changed since his graduation on this very spot 14 years ago. That is, except for the body lying in the middle of the grass-covered dais, The Cistern.

The large raised oval was a centerpiece at the small South Carolina college and was the platform for graduations, concerts, gatherings, and film locations like *The Patriot* and *Cold Mountain*.

Not bloody corpses.

He was back in Charleston where he'd known who he was. The place before New York. And Nadia. And the authorities. And ultimately, obscurity.

Two hours ago he set out on an early morning cross-campus stroll when he found the nasty scene. Not the kind of thing you'd expect to find in a pre-dawn walk down memory lane. He was en route to a second chance at his career and dealing with the police again was not on his list of things to do today.

"What've we got here?" Jack followed the voice to a man walking toward the scene with an "I'm in charge now," attitude.

The entire lawn area was roped off with police tape. Students lined the sidewalk, gawking through the wrought iron fence that separated St. Philip Street from campus. A photographer from The Post and Courier was shooting from outside the tape on the far side of the lawn as a reporter chatted with students and lookers-on. Jack recognized the photog as Dan Banyon. They'd been in a class together at The College of Charleston and had become friends. They hadn't been in touch for years. Maybe he'd call him later today, maybe get together for a beer.

The victim, a young man, lay face up at dead center. Dead being the operative word. His arms and legs spread out on the grass like he'd been making snow angels. His throat gaped a red slit.

There was blood, but the ground had soaked up some of it. And the kid would have died almost instantly. Almost. One hand was a crimson glove. The kid had reached for his throat, felt the hot, wet blood squirting out. Jack winced at the thought. Imagine being young and vigorous, and one second later…nothing. The unexpected suddenness of this kid's death struck him and he drew a quick gasping breath much like the one when he'd first seen the body.

A backpack lay near the lifeless feet. It was open, papers hanging out, a lab book a couple of feet away. Looked like the creep who'd done the deed'd been looking for something. Had he—or she—found it?

A trail of ants made a jagged parade along the crimson trail to the student's neck.

"Who found him?" the man in charge asked. An officer pointed toward Jack and he knew it was time for more questions. He stood to meet the officer heading his way.

"Det. Skeet Mallory, Charleston Police Department," the man said, hand extended. Mallory was average height and build, about Jack's age, but with a rumpled appearance.

"Jack Chase." The men shook hands.

"So, you found the victim, Mr. Chase?"

"Yes, just at daybreak." Jack didn't feel the need to say any more than necessary. He knew better than to get too chatty with the police.

"Probably others came by earlier. Probably wouldn't've seen him lying here in the dark. Or if they did, didn't want to get involved," Det. Mallory said glancing around, then making serious eye-contact with him.

An efficient looking uniformed woman approached. Her nametag read "Owens."

"We're canvassing students who might've walked through last night. Running down friends, enemies, priors, the usual drill," said Officer Owens said. "Crime scene crew is doing it's thing."

She flipped through her notepad. "Name's Craig Duncan. Student ID." She held up the baggy containing the blood-spotted student card.

"TOD appears to be midnight, give or take an hour. It didn't get below 88 last night, so it's hard to tell."

Jack half-watched as the crime scene guys collected bits of grass, paper, cigarette butts, taped brick pathways vacuumed for fibers and hairs, followed any blood trail from the killer as he exited the scene.

"Let me know what you find," Mallory said, squinting up

at the sun peeking through the old oak trees. "The College dudes are having a cow—and I can count on the Mayor to call before noon," Mallory mumbled half to himself and half to Jack, and Officer Owens.

"We need to move this along—and for crying out loud, get him covered up, will ya," he barked at the woman before turning back to Jack.

Chapter 2

Jack slipped out of the brutal July afternoon into the cool brick entry of Simons Arts Center on the College of Charleston Campus. He swiped the back of his hand across his damp forehead. He was late—but then who would have anticipated the events of the morning.

A woman griped just outside the door about the humidity messing up her hair. Must be from off, not from here, he thought as the door clanked shut on the heat and the whining visitor.

His footsteps echoed off blond oak floors and brick walls as he headed to the exhibition hall on the far side. The long, mostly empty room was just visible through the partially opened door. Inside, a woman, auburn hair curling down her back, examined a man's form standing in the middle of the room. She caressed a chiseled leg, traced her fingers over a well-muscled calf and slipped her hand into the hollow behind a left knee.

Jack's breath held as her hands continued up the torso.

Whoa...

What the hell was she doing? Bare hands on precious marble. He watched as she admired the form, handled it lovingly, caressed the arms, ran her hands flat across the chest. The marble statue stood unmoved by her exploration. Jack, on the other hand, felt every bit the voyeur, and responded as any man would. That and a rising sense of outrage not wanting this amateur to mess up anything that might make the work ahead more difficult or compromise his chance at a future.

He made a step to enter the hall to stop the sacrilege when the door behind him opened with a flourish. Longtime friend Rachel Stover rushed across the lobby to join him. As the college's head of acquisitions and exhibitions she was in a socially visible position at the college. Perfect for her and good for the college's image.

"Jack," Rachel's voice bounced against the walls as she hugged him and planted an enthusiastic quick kiss on his lips.

"Glad you could come on such short notice," she said, referring to the late night phone call two days earlier when she'd pleaded with him to help her with an "unexpected and intriguing project."

"Have you seen it yet?" she asked.

"No...well kinda'...running late...started the morning by finding a murder victim," he said, wincing and relating the highlights to Rachel.

"Good lord," she responded, her tone indicating her lack of interest. She clutched his arm closer to her chest, pasted a smile on her face and asked again if he'd seen the statue.

He cocked his head toward the curtain. "There's some girl in their fondling it. I was about to tell her to get her hands off him," Jack said, a smile pulling his lips slightly to one side.

"That must be Sarah. It's her statue...if finders keepers

13

counts for anything." Rachel said, "which it doesn't in this case." She hugged his arm close to her, flashed blue eyes up at him. Their friendship had survived adolescence, a brief college love affair and years of sparse communication.

She seemed as enthusiastic as ever. Always a little over the top. Fun. Dangerous. And still as beautiful as ever. Blond, sleek hair curved just above her shoulders. Her brilliant aqua eyes the product of strong genes and tinted contacts.

"Let's see what you've brought me all the way to the east coast to see. Lead the way Rache."

But instead of leading the way into the gallery, Rachel pushed him against the rough, brick wall. Her lips tickled his ear as she whispered,

"I'm so glad you could find time to help me out with this. I've missed you, Jack."

Jack twisted his neck away to look hard at Rachel. Always in the midst of intrigue, a temptress, more interested in excitement than in good sense. He kissed her quickly on the forehead.

"Now introduce me to this statue you're so excited about."

Rachel grabbed his hand and led him back to the curtain, brushed it aside and pulled him into the gallery.

The woman looked up from her examination, her face relaxed into a smile, full lips edged with excitement that lit up the stark room. Soft green eyes flashed golden specks—and that hair. It was a riot of auburn curls with red highlights that seemed to move with a life of their own. She was tall, a substantial woman. And beautiful in a very unorthodox way. But something about her...

"It's spectacular, Rachel. How lucky can we be to have a piece like this?" she said, glancing briefly at Jack, then grinning at Rachel before turning her attention back to the headless torso.

The woman's smile practically glowed, her skin flushed with excitement. And she was obviously smitten with the marble man. But Jack was irritated with her for putting her hands on the statue.

All he knew so far was what Rachel had explained on the phone, that her assistant Sarah had found the piece hidden in a basement of one of the oldest buildings on campus, circa 1860s.

"Breathtaking," Jack said, staring at the piece as he walked around it, visually exploring the form situated on a pedestal, pulling on his gloves.

"Sarah, this is Jack Chase, the art expert I told you about," Rachel said.

"Sarah Singleton," she replied, enthusiastically gripping Jack's hand and pumping it heartily. Her smile was dazzling, her southern accent making his own relaxed Charleston brogue seem almost stiff.

"Nice to meet you," he said in a tone just curt enough that the words had an edge.

He refocused his attention on the four-foot tall statue. He pulled a notebook and pen from his leather bag and began taking notes as he continued to survey the piece.

"You do know better than to touch this without gloves, don't you?"

Sarah, flushed, then pulled latex gloves from her pocket and slipped them on over elegant long fingers. So, she did know better than to touch the marble barehanded. What he'd seen earlier was a guilty pleasure. He reached in his pocket to pull out his own latex.

"We haven't found the head," she said, absentmindedly tracing her glove-clad finger up the statue's inner thigh as she and Rachel continued to chat. "It appears to have been

15

deliberately removed, sawed off." She touched the edge of the neck.

Jack moved closer to the statue, a beautiful example of Italian Carrera marble sculpted in the style of the 1600s. For several minutes he explored the piece, a cursory look that made him feel this was authentic. The detail was stunning, the craftsmanship superb. Priceless. A reboot of his career. His pulse raced as his mind leapt forward to the press conferences, the articles he would write, the speaking engagements he surely would be offered. Or would it turn out to be a first-rate fake? Nothing more than a brief in the back of Art & Antiques magazine on how easily people can be fooled by well-executed frauds. He wanted the cover.

The women continued talking, creating background noise as his mind time-traveled to the 17th century. He could hear the mallet and the chisel as the artist chipped away, smoothing the statue into existence. Jack had always felt like he'd been born in the wrong century. He belonged back there. What he wouldn't give to have watched the masters at work. All he could do now was imagine the scene. Raw stone revealing the life within, a figure that could still evoke emotion more than 400 years later.

"Earth to Jack," Rachel teased. Rachels' voice dragged him back to the present.

"Italy circa 1620 or so. If this is a fake, it's a damn good one," Jack said, speaking to Sarah, then, "Thanks for calling me in, Rachel. Even if it's not the real thing, you gotta admire whoever created it. It's in the style of Bernini."

He opened his small case and removed a vial with a dropper top, cotton swabs and several empty test tubes. He swabbed the sculpture where the head had been removed, methodically taking samples from the front and sides of the broken surface and putting them individually in the empty test tubes, stoppering them and sliding them back into the case.

"I'll send these off to the lab for any trace materials that might help us," he said efficiently.

He looked again at the sculpture, sighed contentedly at the work he knew was ahead…the kind of mystery he lived to unravel. It'd been a long time since anything provoked the feelings he had right this minute: a puzzle to solve and two beautiful women.

Chapter 3

Sarah knew she was basically obsessed over the statue. But she didn't care. The crate was opened two days ago, on the 12th anniversary of her arrival in Charleston, the day her real life began. The life she'd chosen for herself. And now she could add another beginning to celebrate on her special day.

The statue. When the workmen came to her office that day and asked her what to do with all the junk they'd found in the basement, she'd first told them to trash it, but then the workman asked,

"What about the statue? That too?"

She followed them back to the basement where they showed her the boxes, barrels and a large crate. She instantly became mother bear to every piece.

The cache of goods, hidden behind a false wall, revealed by the long overdue renovation of Randolph Hall, included several trunks packed with clothing, barrels of dishes, a few pieces of furniture—and the now half-opened crate containing the statue.

"Sarah? What do you think?" She was dragged back to the here and now, and a professional art detective who could possibly shed light on her find. Rachel described Jack as a man who knew more about sculpture and antiquities than nearly anyone in the world. Sarah watched as he examined the marble. He seemed excited, interested.

"Is it real?" she asked anxiously as she monitored his cursory examination of the statue. She shadowed his every step. "It looks real to me, but I really don't know all that much. Just what I've read," she chattered away, knew she was babbling. She wanted this to be the best thing that anyone, anywhere, had ever found.

"Well?" she asked impatiently, squinting into the spotlight. Jack Chase was tall, but she'd not yet gotten a good look at his face. He had great hair. Light brown, long enough to be interesting but short enough to take him seriously. He had an elegant, yet haunted look about him.

"It'll take more than a quick look," he said without turning to speak, his voice deep but soft. He was absorbed in his work. "Did you say you found this in a basement?"

"Right. It was behind a false wall with stacks of trunks and dish barrels."

"Excellent. I'll need to see all of that," Jack said efficiently.

She'd supervised the move of the artifacts to a storage shed behind the arts building after the renovation site manager, Dirk Atkinson, ordered "that old stuff" removed from the area.

Sarah protested, but Atkinson lacked any interest in Southern history—not to mention art—and he'd been given complete control of the renovation. And he had a deadline.

In addition to being more enamored of a blue print than he was Civil War artifacts, Atkinson was from someplace "up north." He was, as the locals said, from "off." That made him practically a non-person here in this city where lineage meant a whole lot more than it should have.

Atkinson had reiterated his orders to the workmen, waved her aside and told the workmen to get that crap out of the way and to quit wasting time. He was under contract to complete the work by the start of school in four weeks. He muttered to himself as he stomped up the stairs and out of view.

Sarah'd taken 100s of photos of the site before she let the men move the first item. Chase wouldn't have the undisturbed area to examine, but at least he'd have the photos to rely on for possible clues. She repeatedly urged the workmen to be careful. She was the caretaker to every item that was found and she took it as her personal and professional responsibility to see that each piece was cared for properly.

But standing here in the exhibition hall was the prize from that find.

The statue.

Chapter 4

Until the day of the discovery, Sarah'd seen herself as just slightly more worldly than the 18-year-old girl who'd left the hills of the Great Smoky Mountains looking for the life she'd hoped for. Her dream felt big to her, although she knew by anyone else's standards, it was probably very small.

But she persevered and made her little dream real.

She grew up rural and disconnected from the rest of the world, even though the family farm was only 20 minutes from Asheville. The city was a long established mecca for artists, cultural pursuits, rich retirees. Yet her universe was so different it could have been on another planet. It was easy to get lost in the valleys and hilltops of the Smokies, and her family had done just that. They isolated themselves from all but the inhabitants of a few nearby farms. Her one friend, Caleb, joined the Army leaving her deserted. Her mother had "known" he wouldn't return. She had "the sight," the one gift her mother had that her father and brothers couldn't touch.

It'd been passed down through the women of her mother's family. Her grandmother had it and was well known for her abilities. But Sarah had never felt the "sight." She'd feared Caleb would die, but had believed he would return to her. When Caleb died "over there," Sarah's devastation was complete, and her lack of the "sight" was confirmed in her own mind.

Her move to Charleston had been an act of survival.

She packed her two pieces of aqua blue Samsonite luggage, purchased for $4.50 at the Goodwill. She caught the Greyhound bus on the side of Dix Creek Chapel Road. The bus hauled her and her secondhand suitcases filled with the few clothes she'd deemed suitable for her new life, to the AmTrak station in Asheville.

She was the oldest of four. As the first-born she was an initial disappointment to her father, a sentiment he expressed time and again. His subsequent joy at fathering three boys was often mentioned.

Her days were filled with the endless care and feeding of animals, the tending of gardens, canning and cooking. She and her brothers had been home-schooled at first, then later attended the small rural school 20 miles away, an hour and a half on the school bus round trip.

"It worked out fine," her father said more than once, as she and her mother cooked the huge meals that were everyday fare at the Singleton table.

"Sister's a big help to Mother—she'd never be able to get enough food cooked for all us menfolk," he'd say, tilting dangerously back in his caned chair and surveying the boys he'd sired. Sarah knew her place. She was kitchen help. But the boys were an obvious source of pride to her father. She took comfort that she'd been a lot of help to her mother, but hers was a lonely life.

Her only respite from solitude was her teacher and the teacher's two children who came to her family's once elegant, rundown house every weekday for music lessons on the twangy piano that had been her grandmothers. The lessons were made possible by her mother sharing her garden produce with the teacher as payment.

On the rare occasions her family went into Asheville, longing and interest broke loose at her first sight of the art galleries, street musicians and coffee houses.

Tourists and locals dined at sidewalk tables when the weather was good. She imagined herself sitting at one of those tables with friends, or with a boyfriend, talking about books or movies.

She caught bits of conversation as she and her family passed by, usually en route to the hardware store for nails or a tractor part.

These trips to civilization were all the more special because of their rarity. Glimpses at lives so different from hers sparked endless daydreams. She stored up aromas from the French bakery and the Italian restaurant, the happy sounds of music from cafés snuggled into old buildings, the colors and places that reached out to her from the paintings hanging in the galleries—and the people, always the people, in their fashionable clothes living their interesting lives. Later her senses recalled the whole scene to relive over and over, to elaborate on, to embellish and create her own characters. To imagine the excitement of conversation about something other than the latest cornbread recipe or how many calves they would have come spring.

"The work is one of heartache, yet hope..." she heard a man say one day as she passed a coffee house. He sat sipping from a

ceramic mug, probably thrown by a local potter. His clothes spoke of casual ease and sophistication as if he'd just put on the first things he'd grabbed from his closet and they'd settled on his frame to form a perfect look. An artist. He looked like what she thought an artist would look like: handsome with dark brown hair curling just over the suede collar of his coat. She'd kept her eyes on him, watching carefully while her family waited for the streetlight to change. It was only a few seconds, but she knew he was the kind of man she wanted. Casual and complicated, but manly and comfortable with himself. Not the kind of man who thought art was a silly female pursuit. Not the kind of man who would tell her reading was a waste of time or that appreciating beautiful things was a sin.

She wrote about her artist that night after the house settled and the sounds of sleep played as background music to her thoughts. *Heartache yet hope.* That was her. Full of both. She swore to herself that when she was old enough she would find a way to have a life of cafés, coffee and conversation about art and literature.

She hadn't meant to leave home when she did, but as it turned out, the timing was just right.

At dinner one night, just a few days before her 14th birthday, her mother asked her what gift she wanted. That was an unusual question. Gifts weren't a usual part of their lives. She was a little taken off guard and blurted out without thinking, "I want to go to college."

Her mother's eyes jerked wide open and her father started yelling about how women didn't need an education "'cause they'd just get married and have babies anyway." Besides, her job was already figured out. She was the oldest and the smartest. She'd be the one to help keep the farm going. She'd learn how to do the books, and order the seed and calculate the prices.

She didn't argue. She wasn't really even all that upset because she'd made up her mind she was leaving home before the words detailing the future he had in store for her were out of his mouth. It was as if someone had flipped a switch. And when the light came on, Sarah knew what she would do. She started making her plans that night. She pulled out a piece of newspaper she'd tucked in her dictionary. Her Pa had brought The Citizen-Times newspaper into the house one day for an advertisement of a farm auction in a neighboring county. There was equipment going on the block that he wanted. Mama had clipped the coupons and studied the food advertisements. When the paper was finally thrown in the waste bin, Sarah retrieved it and read around the holes, taking in every word, including the remaining advertisements. There was a story about the College of Charleston, about a new library being built there. Pictures of the campus illustrated the beauty the article described. She knew Charleston was the right place for her. She was drawn to the city like iron to a magnet.

She fell in love that night with the idea of going there. With the idea of leaving home. With the idea of having her own life. She would go there and learn about art and maybe even writing. She knew it would be hard but she didn't care. She had four years to make it happen. She started saving her money a few pennies at a time in a small wooden box she hid behind the baseboard in the corner under her bed.

For two years, her plan sustained her, but then, the unthinkable happened. Her mother became pregnant and Sarah's life was put on hold. Her mother, her only ally in the world, and the one person who supported her need to learn and to move on, no longer had the energy to do more than exist. Her mother became weaker and weaker. Sarah tried to shoulder the load, doing all the cooking and gardening, missing as much school as she dared without having to repeat a grade. And finally deciding that was exactly what would have to happen. One day her mother noticed she'd been home from school three days that week.

"Don't do this, Sarah," she'd said as she grabbed her arm and locked her eyes with Sarah's. "You have to leave here. Promise me." She wouldn't let go until Sarah nodded "yes."

"I have a little money saved for you. It's in the henhouse under the stone."

The situation worsened as the days passed, and her mother seemed to dissolve before Sarah's eyes. When she and the baby died in childbirth, Sarah was devastated and cried more tears than she knew were possible. Her mother was gone.

She couldn't think about the future and felt the trap was set that would keep her in this house, caring for her father and brothers. She didn't check under the stone for her mother's money. She couldn't. Not yet anyway.

But just as fate had ended a life and a dream, fate interceded again. Within six months, her father came home with a new wife. A woman not much older than Sarah and a woman not interested in sharing her kitchen with a stepdaughter.

Leaving actually turned out to be a whole lot easier to do than she figured it would be. The hard part had been finding the courage and resolve to go. She checked bus schedules and ticket prices. She went to the bloodstone where the chickens' bodies, amidst much flapping and squawking, were separated from their heads. She searched the soil around the edge of the weathered granite and found a place that had not been packed and caked tight by years of blood and weather. When she dug there, she found a Del Monte green bean can, the old kind that were actually made of tin. Inside were dollar bills, molded in spots, yellow-orange with rust from the seams of the can. There was $173 in all. It was a fortune. Combined with her own cache earned from weeding the neighbor's garden, it would be more than she'd ever seen before in one place, $247.56. That money would make the difference between staying on the farm and going to Charleston. She applied for scholarships, asked teachers for letters of support that they happily gave her. She had enough to at least get started out of town. After that it would be up to her to make her own way and create a new reality. The one thing she knew for sure, she did not want the life she'd come from. Her mother's life. Her beautiful, sweet mother.

And she'd done it.

Sarah had not gone home to the mountain for five years, and then only to see her grandmother as she lay on her deathbed. She held her hand, told her how much she loved her.

"You have the gift Sarah," her grandmother said in little more than a whisper. "Trust yourself, do not fight against it as you always have, and believe what I say. You are destined for a great love, and you will have an important life."

At the funeral, Sarah looked across the gravesite at her father and brothers. They seemed the same, and she thought she was the same. During lunch a few hours later, she sat at the weathered picnic table, enjoying familiar tastes of field peas and potato salad from Mrs. Granger, Aunt Sue's baked beans. Caleb's mother's fried chicken. The food elicited the usual murmurs of appreciation. But the men of her family seemed distant, a little nervous. Not hostile, but not welcoming either. Sarah didn't recognize the changes in herself until she felt the reaction of her family on her return.

"I'm surprised you came back at all to the old place. You look city-like," her father said. Only through their eyes did she see herself in a new way. She was becoming the woman she hoped someday to be. Her younger siblings, now adult men in the mold of their father, were much as they had been. Her father, too, was much the same, although his new young wife, now pregnant, looked a little worse for wear.

The wake and funeral were brief and Sarah's departure abrupt. As soon as lunch concluded, she asked Caleb's father to drive her to the Asheville train station in Biltmore Village. Momma'd been gone five years by then and Sarah'd graduated from the College of Charleston with honors. In all that time, her father had never contacted her. She sent cards at birthdays and Christmas; her calls to check on her brothers were met with monosyllabic responses.

Her life before Charleston had become little more than a sad memory.

Chapter 5

Sarah led the way across the gravel parking lot to the storage shed as Jack Chase followed.

"So when did you find this exactly?" he said suddenly breaking the silence between them.

"Two days ago," she responded without turning to look back. Gravel crunched under their feet.

"The workmen doing the renovations came to me and asked where to dump it. Can you imagine?" She smiled back at him, knowing instinctively he would appreciate how barbaric the workers were to even suggest such a thing.

"I had them move it here when the renovation manager said it had to go. I took photos of the scene to record as much as possible. I really haven't slept much since then."

"I haven't either…since Rachel called and asked me to check it out. And thanks for taking the photos. Not everyone would have thought to do that."

She detected an earnestness in his voice and turned to offer him a smile. "I'm hoping you can help us discover its history," she said.

"So do I," he said as she inserted the key into the padlock, opened the door and flipped the switch, flooding the room with light that revealed dusty furniture and old lamps piled in one corner and Sarah's artifacts stacked up against the far wall.

Adrenalin soared. He could see the future. His future. And it was about to unfold.

Chapter 6

Jack made a quick inventory of the containers. Among them was the crate that once had held the statue. The warehouse sweltered in the humid Charleston heat.

He'd worn a jacket and tie this morning—not his style at all—a concession to his anxiety about returning to Charleston. He slipped the jacket off and shook the edge of his wilted double-starched shirt to billow a little air between him and the pinwale Oxford cloth. It was hot as hell, yet he felt more at peace than he had in years. Despite the grisly discovery this morning, he couldn't be happier to be back in the Holy City among its antebellum homes, moss draped live oaks, vendors and history.

This was work. His work. The kind of work he was good at despite the New York disaster. He would get it right this time.

"This is unbearable," Sarah said. "We better give it another try after the sun goes down. Maybe it'll cool off some."

They practically raced each other out of the sweltering box

into the relative cool of the 90-degree afternoon. He watched as Sarah shook out her soft fiery curls and picked at her blouse to unglue it from her body. He'd forgotten how miserable Carolina summers were. An after-dark cool-down was never a sure thing—the heat trapped in the buildings, roads and heavy damp air acted like passive heaters, yielding their remaining heat to the night air.

His life hadn't been all that swell since he left the South. It'd been fine at first, but life's little miseries soon crept in and chipped away at all that confidence he'd been so filled up with when he left college.

New York. Nadia. Obscurity.

He grew up in Camden, South Carolina among the golden boys, the society crowd of the smaller, inland South Carolina equivalent of Charleston. He lived in what would be considered, by anyone's standards, a really, really big house. Only people who didn't live like he did, referred to his and the houses of his friends as mansions. Girls chased him. When he wanted to get laid, he'd let a Melissa or an Ashley or a Britney catch him. He'd gotten lucky. Many times. But, hey, that's what guys did. At least all the guys he knew. Who'd it hurt—really? The girls got what they wanted, too. Bragging rights to share with girlfriends. It was as much a competition for them as it was an act of nature for the guys.

And it was all he'd ever known. A lifestyle passed down from father to son, yet there was always an unease with all of it.

Camden was historic, cultured—an interesting city where horse racing, quail hunting and art were appreciated in equal measure. Camden still had a strong European influence. Sunday afternoon polo was a regular event with sleek horses and their privileged riders.

Like many of the town's old families, the Chase family

stables contained well-bred horses, some of which had taken a turn on the national circuit. The Springdale steeplechase racecourse had been his playground. The wallpaper of his life had been hedges and fences surrounded by pine forests, eager debutantes, money—and family expectations. Yet he was the outsider, always trying to fit in, never quite comfortable in the skin that was his legacy.

In the two years following high school he aced his classes while screwing every skirt he could get into, drinking every kind of alcohol ever fermented, and trying—at least once—all the drugs de jour. A great little scar at the outside corner of his left eye, a memorial to the day his head bounced off the steering wheel of the Jag during a rear-ender with a horse trailer after the Carolina Cup. But even his scar was blessed—it crinkled slightly when he grinned, adding character to what otherwise would have been merely a handsome face.

Then one morning just short of his 20th birthday, he woke up with one leg draped over yet another blond coed with the boring reality that he'd been there and done that more times than he cared to consider. The future—his future—held no excitement. Nothing to strive for. Nothing that inspired even a hint of passion.

Pleasing his father had been important to him when he was young. He tried to want what his father wanted for him. But as he stood on the brink of adulthood, he knew he could never be happy working in an inherited business that seemed as dull to him as unsweetened ice tea. The older he got, the further the chasm grew between them. He wanted more than an empty marriage that provoked affairs. He wanted more than just a job.

In his boredom, he found himself wandering Columbia, the capital city, rummaging in old bookstores. More often than not he found himself intrigued by art books. He purchased and read them constantly, forgetting some days to go to his accounting classes. The books caused him to search out the few galleries in the city. He studied the artists, he examined technique in paintings at the Columbia Museum. He visited parks where statues stood as perches for pigeons and blackbirds. Who was the sculptor? Where had the stone come from? An obsession was born. He eventually sought out every sculpture he could find. In just a few weeks he'd seen them all, researched endlessly and realized a passion in himself he'd never known.

But he was suffocating in Columbia. It was as if he'd forgotten how to breathe. Or maybe he realized for the first time he'd never really known how. He thought about it a lot while still maintaining his status as a party animal. He threw himself even more devotedly into his studies, but there was no challenge. Business was simple.

The family's heir became the family disappointment. In his junior year, he left the University of South Carolina business school and the MBA his father had expected him to get. He turned his back on the "right" fraternity he'd so easily pledged the day he drove on campus in his Jaguar convertible, a graduation present from proud parents.

"Numbers don't lie," his father always told him.

And they didn't. The figures were there. They were what they were. Where was the mystery?

At the end of his sophomore year he took a trip to Charleston to visit his childhood friend Rachel. Sure he'd been to Charleston many times before, but usually on a drunken weekend with fraternity brothers. This time, though, Rachel shared with him her Charleston. Artists and performers seemed to be everywhere: A troupe of street mimes delighted tourists on the sidewalk near her waterfront condo, a saxophonist staked out a busy corner further down the street, art gallery doors stood open as people strolled the antique city. It was Spoleto Festival and the city ached with aging beauty and throbbed with artistic energy.

He'd taken a deep breath and smiled from his gut. It wasn't New York or Paris. It was better. It was the South. His South. He'd been half in love with Rachel by the time the weekend was over. He later came to realize the city, and not Rachel, had elicited all that emotion. But she'd fallen for him and he was just as happy to be with her as with a stranger. What was it to him? Love was meaningless. He'd seen that in his parents' marriage. Not for him. So he an Rachel became a couple.

A week later he applied to the art history program at the College of Charleston. In July, when his acceptance letter came, he didn't have to decide—he traded in his father's dream for his own. It was the first thing he'd ever truly decided just for himself. Everything else, from his college choice and curriculum, to the fraternity legacy from his father and the car he drove, had been someone else's idea of what he wanted. Even his clothes and shoes came from Shehorn's, the conservative men's store where his father's clothes were purchased; where Jack could go in any time, pick out what he wanted and leave without a single bill or charge slip ever crossing the counter. His purchases would be discreetly added to the family's tab and paid at the end of the month by their accountant.

But acceptance by the college and acceptance by his family were worlds apart. Arguments rocked the family estate for a long, agitated summer. Jack stood his ground. He actually took a job at the racetrack caring for horses. That money along with his bank account—everyone in his family had a bank account—made his junior and senior years at the College of Charleston possible. His mother stood behind him, but let him handle it on his own. At his graduation she presented him with a substantial trust account. It was, after all, her family money that paid for their comfortable life. She wanted to support his career—believed in him, knew he'd be a huge success. Creating another man like Jack's father—someone obsessed with business and the next big deal or acquisition—was not what she wanted for Jack and told him so.

Jack's life in New York was easy because of his mom. Probably too easy. He hadn't struggled and as a result hadn't been as careful as he should have been. He'd been cocky. Nothing could go wrong. He led a charmed existence. He had no reason to believe that would not continue.

When Nadia came into his life, he was already making a name for himself in art circles as one of the best art authenticators in the country. His work for one of the largest auction houses in the world grabbed the attention of those who mattered in the business. He'd been fearless. Why wouldn't he be?

Jack met Nadia at a pre-auction viewing in New York. She'd been watching an Alexander Calder lobster trap and fish tail mobile that twisted in a lazy rotation overhead, her face tilted up, her straight black hair plunging well past her waist and tickling the top of an excellent ass. Elegant features, long legs that went on forever and an aura of mystery had left him dumbstruck. That's what he'd been. He'd dated lots of girls, but this was a woman. And even before he met her he was pretty damn sure her name wasn't Su-Su or Bree or Tippie.

He'd pursued Nadia, but she'd kept him at arms' length. Long nights he would lie in bed thinking about her, wanting her, plotting and planning how to impress her and make her want him. Making solitary love to her before falling asleep.

He was frantic with desire.

Just when he thought he couldn't stand it anymore she gave into him, setting the trap, he later realized. He took the bait. There were trysts in limousines, in the elevator going to her hotel room, an alcove at the Metropolitan Museum of Art. He was in love with her. For the first time he was more interested in pleasing someone else more than himself. Not that he wasn't feeling mighty damned pleased about this affair. He, who had broken more hearts than he could remember, ached like a schoolgirl.

When Nadia asked him if he would authenticate a painting for a friend, he readily did so. He expected the piece to be real. He researched without the objectivity critical to finding the truth. He saw only the facts and clues supporting the theory the painting was authentic. It never really crossed his conscious mind it could be anything other than fabulous and real. *This piece is as real as our love, and as fabulous as Nadia*, he thought the day he wrote up the research and decision on the piece. She told him it'd been a purchase by one of her clients who found it during a trip to a small village in Switzerland. His heart pounded with excitement as he told Nadia—beautiful Nadia—the painting was worth a small fortune. When Nadia said her friend was interested in selling the piece, he recommended it to the auction house to handle.

The auction took place. Hundreds of thousands of dollars changed hands. As soon as the transaction was complete, Nadia and her "friend" disappeared. Gone. Jack searched, a sick suspicion growing deep in his belly.

At first he tried to ignore his conscience, but eventually he asked the new owner of the painting to request another appraiser to examine the piece. When the appraiser deemed it a fake, albeit a good one, the auction house declined Jack's overtures to authenticate subsequent pieces. His desire had colored his judgment and his judgment was the most important skill an appraiser could have. In fact, the only one that really mattered.

Humiliated and still wanting Nadia, he left New York.

After drifting his way up and down the West Coast for the better part of a year he came back east and took a job teaching at a small college in West Virginia. He'd been there since. For five years he licked his wounds and refused to give the art world a thought. He never heard from, or of, Nadia again. The case was still open, but the authorities had no leads and it had slipped from their radar.

When the New York fiasco made the news, his father couldn't resist the opportunity to tell Jack he should have done things "the right way." He tried to talk him into coming back to Camden. He'd find some spot in the company for him.

"Something where you can't do too much damage," dear old Dad had said.

Jack hadn't spoken to his father since. He'd also rejected any relationships with women. There was the occasional night at the movies with the other teachers, but other than that, he wasn't interested. It was like the light had gone out of him. A switch had been flipped.

When Rachel called, he stalled, but she finally talked him into coming to Charleston.

"Come on, Jack. Help me out. This is really important. You're the only one I can trust with this." she cajoled.

He needed to start over. It was summer, between semesters. At the very least, he'd hang out with Rachel in the best little city in the world. This could be a back way into the culture that had closed its doors to him. Maybe he'd find his way home. He reluctantly agreed to come, did not sleep that night and fidgeted through the whole flight to Charleston.

"Where're you staying?" Sarah asked as they walked back across the gravel lot to the gallery. "You'd probably appreciate a chance to get settled."

"Mills House," he responded, pulling the door open for her.

Jack found himself relaxed and smiling. It'd been the right call to come back to the beginning, to a place where he knew who he was. Maybe he *could* start all over again. Rachel and Sarah were both kind and solicitous of his opinion. He felt important for the first time in ages. And Sarah was a congenial girl—-smart, professional, and beautiful in a very southern way. The antithesis of Nadia, yet alike in some indefinable way.

He watched her drift past him through the doorway, her tangle of dark hair bouncing back and forth with each step. The past, the first time he'd seen Nadia, flickered, then was gone before it fully registered as a thought. A slight chill rushed over his forearms

"I'll drop you off at the hotel and come back after dark and we'll go to the shed."

Before making his way into the lobby, Jack watched Sarah disappear into the sluggish traffic of Meeting Street in her little convertible. She was nothing like Nadia. Then why did this girl remind him of her? He couldn't keep his eyes off her. His good sense screamed "stay away."

This statue was his big chance. He didn't intend to get derailed again.

The elevator in the old hotel was brass, wood and achingly slow. As it ground to a stop on the third floor, Jack smiled at the memory of one debauched night in this hotel with a couple of sorority girls who'd been just as smashed as he'd been. It could've been a hundred years ago, but in reality had been less than a decade. How could he ever have been that person?

The phone rang as he unlocked the door, pushed it open, dropped his suitcase next to the bed and picked up.

"Hi there, Jack." It was Rachel. "I'm downstairs. What room are you in?"

He looked at the still open door. "312."

"I'm on my way up."

Jack's stomach growled. He'd planned on room service and time alone to make a few notes before going back to the shed. Oh, what the hell? He wouldn't even be here if it wasn't for Rachel.

"I'll be wai…" he was saying when the receiver went dead. He left the door open while he unpacked and dropped his man-bag of shaving gear in the bathroom.

A few minutes later he looked up to see Rachel standing in the doorway.

"Hi handsome," she said, leaning against the doorframe holding a bottle of wine in one hand and two glasses in the other. "I took the liberty of ordering room service for us. They said 30 minutes. And I say that gives us just enough time to get reacquainted."

For him, the romance had been over for years. He was counting on her friendship, nothing more.

"Aren't you going to ask me in?" she continued her seduction.

Sure he was. Rachel was one of the best parts of his past and he was, after all, chasing the past. Despite the messy breakup, she'd kept in touch and maintained their friendship.

He walked over to her and stood within an inch, looking

down into her brown eyes and languid lips for a full five seconds.

Heat built in the slim space between them. His blood churned old stirrings to life. His breath quickened and despite his better judgment, he whispered down into her upturned face.

"Come on in."

Chapter 7

Water trailed down Sarah's back, sluiced over her hips and sheeted off her calves. The cool shower felt wonderful, but she didn't linger. Her enthusiasm ran high, blood pulsed. It would take more than a project manager with an attitude and an overheated shed to snuff out her passion for the challenge ahead. This could be the one moment in her life where she could rise above mediocrity. She could actually become someone of substance in the art history field.

She grabbed the thick white towel and dried off, took momentary stock of her body in the bathroom mirror: breasts a little small, hips a tad big, waist about right. *Could be worse*, she concluded as she tried to brush some order to her hair before pulling it back in a ponytail band.

A dab of lipstick and mascara were enough. Anything more would just melt off in the heat anyway. She was excited, yes she was. She had a few minutes before time to pick up Jack Chase. The expert. He was handsome, but a little intense for her taste. *Who in the world wears a suit in this kind of weather? Oh well, it takes all kinds.* And honestly she was a little embarrassed he'd seen her touching the statue barehanded. She didn't know what had come over her—but the desire to actually feel the stone had overwhelmed her good sense and training.

She'd watched him in her rear view mirror as she pulled away from the curb of the Mills House. He stood there on the sidewalk looking manly and little-boy-lost all at once. As she turned off Meeting onto Queen she saw him walk into the hotel.

He'd been a surprise. Rachel described him as preppie, brilliant—a friend from her childhood. Sarah had joined Rachel at her family's home in Camden before and knew what her childhood meant. She still hadn't gotten over the lifestyle and privilege that came with the kind of money Rachel's family and friends had. A different universe. Jack came from that, too. But he seemed different from Rachel. There was more there. And he seemed so physically uncomfortable. He kept adjusting his tie, and shirt.

She found herself looking forward to eight-thirty in part because of the work ahead, but also because she wanted to find out more about Jack. She zipped herself into her cropped jeans, slipped into a light knit top and grabbed the phone. She dialed Rachel. No answer. She left a message. The rest of the story on Jack Chase would have to wait.

She headed for the door when the phone rang. *Probably Rachel.*

"Hello," she said. There was no answer. "Hello?" She waited a couple of seconds and hung up. But she was sure someone had been there.

Chapter 8

Sarah pulled her British racing green Miata onto Queen Street and into a space an SUV couldn't even dream of occupying. Street parking in downtown Charleston was a challenge that most days rose to the level of sport and she wasn't a big fan of the concrete behemoth parking garages and their hollow echoes.

As always on hot, clear evenings, she left the top down on her tiny car and headed for the hotel half a block away.

Dark cooled the city leaving a damp but almost pleasant 85 degrees in its wake. Gas lamps flanking The Mills House hotel entrance flickered gold against the salmon stucco building as the doorman bid her good evening. The lobby was relatively quiet. Her steps echoed on the white marble-tiled floor. Tantalizing aromas of grilling meat wafted in from the hotel's restaurant kitchen.

"Jack Chase," she said to the desk clerk.

"Yes ma'am, I'll call his room." The clerk handed her the receiver.

"Hello," his voice was strong.

"Mr. Chase?"

"Yes?"

"It's Sarah Singleton. I'm downstairs. Are you ready?"

In the background she heard a woman's voice. Playful banter in the background. *So. He watches sitcoms?*

"That's Jack," he corrected, "And I'll be right down." Again, female laughter trickled through the receiver as the connection clicked off.

Within minutes, he joined her in the lobby. His light brown hair, instead of slicked back in the austere look he'd affected that morning, now hung in a loose wave, shaping his face and brushing the edge of a black t-shirt. She was suddenly a teenager in Asheville, watching the man at the street café.

"Ready to roll?" he smiled down at her, slung a small leather backpack over his shoulder, and took her arm.

"Lead the way, Miss Sarah." His demeanor was casual, fun. His jeans perfect.

She pointed the way. Within minutes they were chatting easily as she pulled away from the curb and threaded her way through the narrow one-way streets. The evening air blew warm against her face, caressing her brow, soothing her with the sheer pleasure of its touch. It was a perfect moment, full of promise as the two of them headed for the shed to discover what clues the contents held to the statue's past.

The answers could be big enough to change her future. Or the entire discovery could be inconsequential, of little value...and that would be okay, too.

Sarah was happy with the little life she'd carved out of a miserable past. But she hadn't lost her dream of a real career.

Chapter 9

They propped the door open with an old cinder block they found wedged against a nearby fence and flipped on the solitary bulb hanging on a bare cord from the ceiling. Sarah squinted in the sudden light as she crossed the room and pushed up a window on the back wall. The release of the hot, stale air made way for a tepid breeze pushing in from the parking lot. Her pulse pounded adrenaline as Jack hoisted the lid off one of the oak dish barrels.

"I need more light," he muttered, fishing a small flashlight from his backpack. The beam dissolved the shadows cast by the naked bulb.

"Beautiful," he said as he pulled on gloves and lifted a plate with intricate scenes of ladies in a courtyard rimmed by a design of roses and butterflies. "A mid-19th century Japanese Imari," Jack said, turning the soup bowl over and inspecting the back. Looks like it came from the Arita area. Unusual. Excellent condition...the owners had good taste," Jack said.

He smiled as he picked up another piece.

Imari was a popular import to the States, he explained distractedly, almost as if she were a student in his class.

"Has anyone else handled these contents already?" he asked, mesmerized by the porcelain.

"No. We thought it best to wait for the expert."

"Thanks. Really. Sometimes important clues are lost—like this," he said, holding up a newspaper scrap. While most of the dishes had been painstakingly stored in cheesecloth, the top two pieces—a cup and saucer—were protected in The Charleston Mercury.

"Looks like whoever was storing these probably ran out of cloth and grabbed the newspaper to finish the job." He pulled a plastic storage bag from his pack and carefully placed the newspaper in it.

"March 20, 1864," he said squinting at the faded print in the inadequate light. "A report on the Hunley's attack on the Houssatonic." We'll read all of it later," he said. She watched as he placed the newspaper into a plastic baggy, labeled it and put it aside on a nearby table. He eagerly opened another container and took preliminary notes in preparation for a complete inventory.

"These need to be moved from here. This heat could ruin the clothing...and this isn't very secure," he said, pointing to the flimsy door and padlock. "Anyone with a crowbar could do more damage than the siege of Charleston ever did."

"I'll talk to Rachel about a better space for it in the morning," she said. Her watch read 10:30. It was late, but she didn't feel at all tired. And she was happy to discover Jack Chase to be congenial company and as intent on the work as she was.

"Did I hear my name being taken in vain," a voice from

the doorway sounded out of place in this makeshift shrine to the past.

Sarah and Jack, startled, turned to see Rachel.

"Rachel! We were just talking about you. Can these be moved into the main building?" Sarah asked.

"I should ask Atkinson, but, what the hell. We can move this stuff right now. Jack? Can you come with me? I know where we can get a hand truck. Sarah, you stand guard. We'll be right back," Rachel said, taking charge.

Jack shrugged at Sarah, grinning, and let himself be dragged out the door by Rachel. They disappeared into the dark. Their voices trailed off, eventually swallowed up by the night sounds of the city.

The shed was suddenly quiet. A faint strain of music floated in the distance. Probably from the park. Performers took advantage of the foot traffic, playing to a constantly shifting audience of tourists and students walking to and from hotels, events and bars.

This was a welcome opportunity to be alone with the past. She rubbed her hand across the top of an old trunk sitting unopened. Worn leather straps were in reasonably good shape. She strained to lift the heavy lid, finally revealing fancy clothing tenderly folded in now-brittle paper by someone long dead. Who was the owner? Only a woman would have taken so much care to save the beautiful clothes and dishes. And the statue? Had that been hers, too? The last time she felt this excited was waiting for the train the day she left Asheville. Anticipation of good things to come mixed with the uncertainty something could wreck her plans.

Sarah pulled on gloves and traced the edge of the satin ribbon of what appeared to be a dress, still warm from the shed's midday heat. She imagined the woman who may have worn it. She ran her hand down the inside panel of the trunk and fingered through layers of clothing as she groped toward the bottom, lightly exploring the contents without disturbing anything. She knew she shouldn't touch it, but good sense didn't seem to apply to anything about the find.

She felt what might have been a buckle, then lace, thin leather—maybe slippers. Her curiosity ran wild but she restrained herself from plowing through the trunk.

When her hand hit something solid, she thought at first she had hit the bottom, but realized she was stopped inches short of the floor. She traced her index finger over the surface and decided it was a small box. Restraint completely deserted her and she gently pulled the box out from the layers, lifting it from its hiding place. Her mind flipped back to Asheville, to the box she'd hidden behind the baseboard in her bedroom. The box that had been the means by which she came to be here, in this shed, holding yet another box. She sat on the floor, looked towards the door and heard nothing, and opened the small, hinged engraved wooden box.

Inside was a tiny key on a ribbon. She held it to the light to examine the engravings on the key. "Diary," it read. *A diary.* She felt carefully through the layers in the trunk, but did not hit on anything that could be a book.

She looked across the room at the plastic container of items the workmen had tossed when they tore down the wall and discovered the stash. Books, bric-a-brac, harnesses, a skillet and a man's hat—obvious last minute additions to the cache that had been hidden behind the wall. She and Jack had not looked through them yet.

She rummaged carefully through the plastic bin, looking at each book and becoming very excited when she lifted one that she at first thought to be a ledger and discovered it had a small lock on it. The diary. She slipped the key into the lock and turned it—the latch opened easily.

She glanced to the door, listened for footsteps, and heard only the subtle hoo-hoo of an owl and the clicking of palmetto fronds. She opened the book and sat on the floor next to the trunk.

Another quick glance at the door, and she turned the first page as if she were unleashing the secrets of the universe. Her heart banged against her ribs. She knew it wasn't rational, but it was as if her whole life, even her reason for coming to Charleston in the first place, had brought her to this moment.

In elegant handwritten lettering was the name, Charlotte Elizabeth. Beneath the name read, "Begun in the Year of Our Lord, January 1, 1863." A coldness settled on Sarah, blocking out everything around her, insulating her from the present, taking her to the past of more than 150 years ago. Mesmerized, she traced the letters with her finger.

And then she turned the first page.

"This is the beginning of my 18th year and it is so filled with the anticipation of...."

The crunch of gravel under approaching footsteps brought Sarah back to the shed. She had the diary halfway back to the bin when she pulled away and tucked it in her purse instead. She placed the wooden box that had contained the key under the first layer of clothes and closed the trunk lid as Jack and Rachel returned pushing a hand truck. She dropped the key down her bra.

"Miss us?" Rachel giggled.

"I kept busy," Sarah said, getting to her feet and brushing the dust from the seat of her jeans. The three worked for the next hour carting the containers into a small room almost directly below the gallery where the statue stood. The room had been a small pottery studio—a table and wheel still inhabited one corner. Clay spatters decorated the space. The room wasn't large, but adequate. The table offered a working space for examining the contents. A stack of tarpaulins on a nearby shelf would work to cover the less than hygienic worktop and keep the materials clean.

Jack Chase was as delighted as a child with a great Christmas toy. His enthusiasm added to her own.

"Well, I've had enough," Rachel said breaking Sarah's thoughts.

Sarah had not had enough. She could work all night. The draw she felt earlier when she first held the diary lingered. It was a familiar feeling. The same feeling she had the first time she saw the newspaper ad about the College of Charleston. It was a longing that could not be denied. A need that came from some place she didn't understand, yet was as real as the diary itself. She thought of her grandmother, her abilities.

Jack winced, "I'd like to stay a little longer."

"Come on, Jack. All work and no play ..."

"Really Rachel, I'm going to stay a little longer. You go ahead."

Rachel pouted.

"I'll stay," Sarah interjected. "I can take you back to the hotel when you're finished," she said to Jack. His pleasure at having an ally was obvious.

Rachel shrugged, grabbed his hand, placed a key in his palm and closed his fingers over it.

"Lock up when you leave." Then she got up in Jack's face and said, "Call me."

It was more than a request. It was an order. Rachel didn't

wait for an answer, but turned and left without another word. The comfortable atmosphere was momentarily broken as Rachel's footsteps ground against the gravel.

After a beat of silence, Jack said, "Let's get back to work."

In the distance the bells of St. Michael's chimed midnight.

And in the background, the traffic played on, tree frogs croaked, and music drifted on the warm, salty breeze as the sound of Rachel's steps echoed into the night.

Chapter 10

Rachel was on the hunt, and Jack was the hunted. He recognized it because he'd been there before. This was exactly the way their first relationship had started, but back then he was too young and ignorant—not to mention drunk and perpetually horny—to see it for what it was. He didn't have that excuse this time—except for the physical need—he hadn't come up with any way or desire to be rid of that part of his nature. Although for the last few years it had lain dormant, he knew it was there, just hidden away under the surface, waiting to reappear. He hoped.

Experience was a great teacher. But just because he had a past didn't mean he understood what relationships were about now. In fact, when it came to emotional relationships with women, he was practically a virgin. He also knew now all his running around had been a defense against getting close to anyone. He'd had plenty of time for introspection in the last five years.

He'd been able to put a stop to Rachel's advances before things went too far yesterday. He'd been tempted at first, but had pleaded exhaustion and distraction about the murder scene that morning. It had in fact been nibbling at the back of his mind all day and knew the morning would require a visit to the police station for a statement. An unexpected phone call from his mother, followed by Sarah's arrival in the lobby soon after, interrupted Rachel's assault and made it possible to get away without much discussion.

As for Rachel, he'd make her realize he was her friend—and that was all they could ever be to each other. His phone again rang as he got back to his room. Two a.m. *Only one person that could be.* Rachel. She wanted to come over. He promised he'd see her in a few hours...at the college. She reluctantly agreed, but let him know she wasn't a bit happy about being put off.

He tossed through the night, partly in anticipation of the next day's work, partly in dread of dealing with Rachel, partly because of the image of the dead student, and curiously, because he was looking forward to working with the very bright Sarah Singleton again.

Chapter 11

*A*n oldies rock station played from a dust-covered radio on the corner shelf as Jack examined the worn coin. Sleep hadn't come easily after the phone call from Rachel. She tried her best to entice him into a late night visit. And he knew it could've been uncomfortable had she succeeded.

Rachel was acting much as she had as a teenager. She thought he was frustrated at not being able to have her. She was mistaken. The only thing he felt was relief at escaping her advances. When she said she'd come down with him, he'd been curiously embarrassed at the idea Sarah would know they'd been upstairs together.

"You're right," she crooned in his ear. "It's better to wait, build the tension. Has a naughty feel to it." She rubbed his leg, kissed him passionately and left by the back way.

He'd talk to Rachel today. The job was more important to him than anything or anyone. He looked at his watch and turned up the volume on the vintage, dusty radio sitting on the shelf next to the bench. "My Girl," crooned from the local 102.5. It was great to be back in the South where the shag was the state dance and the sea air hung over the city in a perfect mix of heavy, magnolia musk and earthy pluff mud.

He was home.

Sarah should be here by now.

He turned the coin over in his hand—definitely pre-Civil War.

"My Girl..." he sang. He liked to sing when he was alone, belting out a tune in a small room. The echo made it sound way better than it actually was. Placing the coin on the tarp he'd spread out on the counter, he picked up the next one as he sang along with the radio. His body naturally fell into the song's rhythm. He'd been doing the shag since he was old enough to walk. His mother'd taught him.

He turned the coin over in his hand. It was different from the other one. Italian. 1853 was the strike date. *"My Girrlll,"* he sang aloud, executing a perfect pivot on one foot to find himself facing a tangle of dark hair and a smiling face.

"Am I interrupting," Sarah said, brilliant smile making him a little weak-kneed and embarrassed to be caught. He laughed and took a bow.

"Thank you, thank you very much," he said in his best Elvis imitation. Sarah applauded his efforts as she came into the room.

"Very nice. So do you sing for your supper when you're not busy doing hotshot art appraisals?"

"Not hardly," he said, holding the coin up between his latex clad thumb and forefinger.

"Wow," she said. "May I?" she asked, tentatively reaching for the coin.

"Sure," he said. She pilled on her gloves and carefully took it and looked it over. "I wonder who the last person was to hold this before us?" she said.

He was touched by her desire to know the people who'd packed the trunks. He'd always been more interested in the physical history of the pieces, but already he was beginning to see this find through her eyes. The humanity behind what they were looking at.

"I don't know...but maybe we'll be lucky enough to find out."

There was a moment of silence that threatened to get uncomfortable. She handed the coin back to him, reverentially. With a flicker of a look into his eyes—light brown she noticed—she moved forward to the table to view the other pieces he'd laid out.

"May I touch these," she asked, looking back over her shoulder.

"Sure...no problem." He started breathing again and joined her at the table.

His unease. Was it the faint resemblance to Nadia? It was getting worse by the second. He reached for a satchel to his left and lifted it onto the worktable. He took another deep breath and tried to clear his mind. What was that scent? *Oh, man.* Her perfume was subtle, almost not there, but enough to do him in. The perfume. Was that it?

"Let's look through this," he said a little louder than he needed to. The small piece looked like a lady's traveling case, with a needlepoint of a cardinal sitting on a dogwood branch. The case was no larger than an oversized present-day purse. Something a late 19th century woman might have carried on a train or stagecoach.

He opened the bag. Inside were small stacks of letters tied in neat bundles with satin bits of ribbon. Pink, lavender, deep blue, pale green—each with the same neat bow on top.

"Jackpot," he said under his breath.

They stood and stared for a few seconds then looked at each other before turning their gaze back to the case and its contents.

"Looks like we really might find out who owned this stuff," she said almost in a whisper.

"Looks like it," he said reaching to lift the bundle tied in lavender ribbon. He held the fragile stack of letters carefully then looked at Sarah.

"I'm not sure this is the right place to go through these. We need a cleaner environment and I need to process the rest of this material," he said glancing around the room at the boxes, barrels and cases stacked on the floor and table. He took the bundles of letters and put each bundle in a separate large baggy and replaced them in the case.

"Then I guess we'd better get busy," she said, moving into action and closing the satchel.

"The sooner we get through this," she said waving her arm in an arc at the work piled up before them, "the sooner we can start in on the letters."

They pulled a barrel over, the one containing the dishes they'd discovered the afternoon before. For two hours, they unwrapped and inventoried each plate, cup and saucer. A service for 12 in a brilliant Japanese design in corals, blues and greens on white china.

Photographs and notes were made and the barrel repacked before they moved on to the next, working methodically and efficiently as a team. The morning had drifted into afternoon when Jack realized someone else was in the room.

He and Sarah both lifted their heads from their work simultaneously to see Rachel watching them from the doorway.

"Rachel," Sarah said brightly greeting her boss.

"Hi guys...busy little bees aren't you?" a note of sarcasm hanging on her words.

"Lots to do," Sarah said.

"Need some help?" Rachel said, sauntering into the room.

For the first time today he felt an unhappy tension seeping into his good spirits. This had been the happiest day he could remember in years. Hopeful. Interested. Last night's phone call from Rachel had unsettled him. She'd pushed and they'd ended the conversation on a tense note. And now she was here.

"Any important finds?" she asked, again with an edge in her voice. He wasn't sure Sarah recognized it, but he sure did. But maybe he was just projecting last night's call onto today's reality.

"You two look pretty cozy," Rachel said, standing right next to Sarah now.

Sarah's look told the tale. She'd definitely picked up on Rachel's attitude and turned back to unwrapping a fork. They'd found a box of silver flatware. "Old Maryland Plain," Jack said. "Engraved with a 'B'."

"I think we're fine right now," Jack said suddenly. "The room is really too small for more than two people." It sounded colder than he meant for it to and it got a rise out of Rachel. He'd handled this badly.

"Sarah. You need to go back to your office. You do have a job you know. And I hate to be harsh, but I am your supervisor and work has to be done. You understand."

Sarah looked like she'd been slapped.

He wanted to leap to her defense, but didn't want to make things worse. "You said yesterday Sarah'd be my official liaison with the college, my assistant. That she would be the one helping with the inventory," Jack said, looking first at the stricken look on Sarah's face and then to Rachel who stood over them with her hands on her hips. But the bottom line was, he didn't really know anything about Sarah.

"She is needed in her office. I'll be glad to help out with the rest of the inventory," she said. "Sarah, Crystal couldn't find the Connor file this morning and she really needs your help to get that project finished."

Sarah stood up face-to-face with Rachel.

"Of course," she said. She looked down, tears brimming in her eyes. He couldn't tell if it was from anger or disappointment.

"Rach…" he started to say more, but Rachel put her hand up for him to stop. "We have a department to run and Sarah is a critical part of our work. She is an extremely important member of our office team. She is a really, really good secretary—excuse me—administrative assistant."

Sarah didn't say a word, but walked from the room without looking back. A door clacked shut, signaling her exit from the building.

"That was outrageous, Rachel. What are you doing? If this is about last night…"

"Don't flatter yourself, Jack. This is strictly business. She has work to do. And you don't know this girl. She's got ways of which you are unaware. I wasn't going to say anything, but she's only here out of the goodness of my heart after what she did."

"What do you mean, 'what she did'?"

"Well there was speculation she had pilfered…stolen…a miniature. But honestly there wasn't any evidence of that. If there had been I would not have kept her on here." Rachel smiled a practiced smile. Her charming smile.

Jack's skin went cold. "Oh." Jack had a sinking feeling.

He wasn't sure how much to believe.

"Draw your own conclusions sweetie. She's a hard little worker. Graduated at the top of her class. Just don't take everything she says as gospel."

"She's the one who found this stuff. She should be allowed to continue working on this project," Jack argued, not quite as enthusiastically as he might have ten minutes earlier.

"I have an office to run. Now let's get busy."

The congenial atmosphere of earlier was gone. In its place was a cold, hard reality. Rachel was Sarah's boss. And was Sarah untrustworthy? Why would Rachel keep her on if she didn't trust her? Regardless, she could make Sarah's life hell. He knew Rachel and what she was capable of. He also could see how much this project meant to Sarah.

He had to find a way to reconcile what Rachel had just told him with the woman who's work on the project so far he'd come to respect.

He and Rachel finished listing the silverware and repacking it. Jack lifted the box onto the worktable and shoved it toward the back, against the wall. As he turned around, Rachel was in front of him, her hands holding the table on either side of him, trapping him. She moved against him seductively.

"Stop it, Rachel."

"Come on, Jack. You know we're good together."

"Rachel. We've been over for years. We're friends. Remember?"

"We are friends. Kissing friends. Friends with benefits— very 'in' these days. You know you want me."

Jack could feel the heat of her body moving against him, working to arouse him. He was not impressed. He didn't want to be with her.

"Rachel. Please. Stop it." He grabbed her by the

shoulders and moved her gently, but firmly away from him.

"It's her, isn't it? The country girl. Wild hair with the big green eyes. She's not your kind, Jack. She'd never fit in with who you are and where you came from."

"I'm not the same, Rache…and this has nothing to do with Sarah," he said, not really believing the last part.

"Bullshit," Rachel said. "Surely you aren't that stupid. She's doing everything she can to get her hooks into you."

"Rachel, listen. You and I've known each other forever."

"Yes. We have known each other…"

"I know we've at times been more than just friends.

"I was beginning to think you had forgotten."

"This is about us. Not her. You were wrong to send her away. It's just plain wrong."

"But that's my decision and not yours. If I see her down here again, I'll fire her." She practically spit the words at him. "And you."

Rachel turned and stomped out of the room. He could hear her footsteps pounding hollowly down the flagstone hallway. A few seconds later the heavy door slammed as she left the building. He stood there, looked at his hands, surveyed the room and its contents. He was suddenly in a barren cage from which he wanted to escape.

"Up on the Roof" played from the radio. A sad smile forced its way to his lips as he flicked the switch to off.

Chapter 12

*S*arah opened her desk drawer, stared blankly into it, and slammed it shut. Rachel's tirade had completely blindsided her. And to be taken off the project—a project that wouldn't even exist had she not cared enough to take a look—was wrong. Rachel would fill the role of working alongside Jack to identify the owner of the stash. But Rachel had no feeling for what Jack was trying to do—for the importance of the work. To Rachel it was just something to do. She knew Rachel liked keeping her under control. Rachel liked having something to hold over people's heads. A power thing.

The statue is everything to me. Everything!

She was frustrated and frantic. It felt like the end of the world to be excluded. In the few short days since it was discovered, the items had become special to her. Almost a reason for her entire being. It was more than a way to move on to a more fulfilling career. It was as if the contents of the trunks and the presence of the statue validated her existence.

The past resonated in the present. She would find a way to be a part of this. She had to. She was meant to. Last night she started reading the diary but after only two pages fell asleep. She was glad now she'd taken it, otherwise it could be weeks before she knew the contents. She only wished she had the letters as well. She and Jack hadn't had time to give them even a cursory inspection before Rachel came in.

A knock on her office door straightened her spine as she stood behind her desk. She brushed her damp cheeks with the back of her hand.

"Come in," she called cheerfully. Crystal, the graduate intern, peeked in the door.

"Hi stranger," she said. "You busy?"

"No. Not at all," she said shuffling a few papers on her desk, putting on a brave front.

Crystal came in and plopped down in the chair opposite her.

"How's the statue?"

Maybe it was Crystal's cheerful smile. Maybe it was because she'd asked about the statue. Or maybe it was that she was operating with little sleep. But all of a sudden, she stood up, and in a fury, picked up a book and slammed it down on her desk scaring Crystal half to death.

"I've been removed from the project," she seethed a hoarse whisper, tears burning her eyes.

"But why?"

"Because I have work to do here in the office. Rachel said you needed me to find a file that was missing."

Crystal stared at her blankly. "What?"

"The file…the missing Connor file that Rachel told me to come find for you."

"I don't know what you're talking about. Everything's fine

here."

"Aaaeeeccchh," Sarah said screeched. She'd already figured there was no office emergency, but had a faint hope there was and that Rachel was justified in ordering her back to her desk.

"I'm going home," she said abruptly, whipping past Crystal as the phone rang. Sarah ran out of her office and down the hall. Why was Rachel acting so badly toward her?

Was it because of Jack? Of the time and the substance of that time they were spending together? But there was no reason for that jealousy. Jack was there to unlock the mystery of the statue. She was there to assist in that effort. Rachel's behavior…seemed wrong even for Rachel.

Sarah wheeled her car from the parking lot and headed down St. Philip Street to Calhoun and over to Meeting Street before veering off on Water Street, the original seawall boundary of the city. A few hundred feet away she made a right onto East Battery and home. She pulled into the driveway, grabbed her purse and stomped across the side yard, through the porch and up the front stairs to her haven.

She shoved the door shut behind her and slung her purse onto the sofa. She'd go up to her refuge, the widow's walk roof. She poured herself a glass of sweet tea, squeezed a wedge of lemon into it, and went into her bedroom to retrieve the diary.

She'd find a way to return it tomorrow, but for now was comforted to have at least this piece of the find to study. She carried it with care. It was part of the city's history, and could have been, should have been, part of her future. She knew this as surely as she knew the harbor waters flowed out with the tide. That the moon would rise over Folly Beach. That the dolphins would follow the sailboats as they sliced through the water. "You have the gift, Sarah," her grandmother's words drifted through the back of her mind.

She ascended the spiral steps to the widow's walk. It was the feature that had sealed her decision to take the third floor apartment. There were two more upstairs units on the second floor, one of which had a balcony with wrought iron railings. Both were studios rented by artists for the expansive windows. The light from the back windows, they said, was perfect. Hers was a little more expensive because of the widow's walk. She had four rooms and a half if you counted the kitchen, bathroom, and a small dressing room she used as her own studio. Her bedroom was roomy and the living area comfortable. Her landlady, Mrs. Harriett Blanding, had offered to give her a break on the rent if she would pick up groceries for her once a week and her medicines as needed. Mrs. Blanding was a semi-invalid and their agreement had worked well for the five years she'd been here. Mrs. B had never taken advantage of Sarah and had been a supportive presence in her life.

Sarah's widow's walk was a joy to her soul and the place where she could imagine other lives, past and present. On summer evenings she watched the boats and container ships as she sipped iced tea and relaxed in her ladder back rocking chair. In the winter she wrapped up in a blanket, cradled a steaming mug of coffee in her hands and watched the moon rise. It was her place to dream, to refresh herself. And on days like this, it was her refuge.

She pushed open the door and stepped onto the rooftop porch with its white balustrade. The top of one tall sabal palmetto tree at the corner of the house draped a few fronds over the railing. As the breeze blew in from the harbor, the fronds clicked like a woody wind chime. Centuries and decades earlier, wives of sailors stood waiting from this and similar rooftop porches all over the city for their husbands to come home from the sea. Sometimes that wait was in vain. Mrs. Blanding's own father had been lost on a merchant ship caught in a storm in the 1930s. Mrs. B's mother had lived the rest of her life grieving and waiting, staring out to sea from her rooftop, praying that by some miracle, her husband would return. Mrs. B herself was unable to do the stairs to get up there anymore and always seemed happy to know that Sarah was making use of the space.

Sarah settled into the heavy wooden chair and breathed in the salt air. In the distance, a cruise ship maneuvered through the jetties into the harbor as deftly as a racehorse outmaneuvering a competitor in a tight pack. Horses...Rachel... Jack... Her momentary escape brought her full circle.

Closer in, fishermen darted around in sleek boats propelled by big engines. A few sailboats dotted the water, making little progress in the light wind. They were a picturesque element on the water's landscape, a reminder that once upon a time, most of the boats on the harbor had been driven by wind. How beautiful that must have been. And how beautiful it was still.

She sipped the lemony tea as her equilibrium fell a little more into balance. Rachel wasn't perfect. So what? She knew that. They'd been co-workers for several years. Friends even. Well, kind of. Friends might be a little strong, but certainly work friends. Granted, when Rachel asked her to go to Camden with her for a weekend, she'd been a little surprised. But it was fun. Rachel had shown off her family's lifestyle and made every effort to offer her a good time.

They rode horses together on winding dirt roads watched over by big houses peaking out from behind high gates, elaborate shrubs and privilege—a buffer between lots of money, inherited entitlement and the rest of the world.

But Sarah was unmoved by it all. Sure it was interesting and entertaining, but she wasn't plagued by pangs of envy. The whole thing had a coldness about it that made her uncomfortable. Rachel's parents were welcoming—but not too much so. There was a reserve she couldn't put her finger on. It was a distance she recognized in Rachel. It was a chasm she would never cross, partly because she had no desire to, but also because the distance was so established between who she was and who they were that to attempt to close the gap was sheer folly. And she knew it. She learned a long time ago the poor of the world saw the distance between the haves and the have-nots for what it was. Unbreachable. And the long-time rich didn't consider it at all. Why would they?

These were the things she pondered as sails flagged on the harbor. She knew her place. And so did Rachel.

Tomorrow she would return to her job in the office and return the diary to the project room. She'd find a way to slip the journal back in among the other papers and books.

And then this whole episode would be done as far as she was concerned. The office. Between writing memos and filing she would plan her future. She would consider it very carefully. And then she would move on. She'd done it before. She could do it again.

But until tomorrow, she would read. She opened the diary of Charlotte Beaufain to read of her hopes and dreams. Descriptions of daily life and visits with friends.

The sails on the harbor are quite beautiful tonight. Father says Charleston is being threatened with another bombardment by the Union. He believes another assault is imminent, and that there is a real possibility that Charleston could fall. But how can one believe such a thing on a night so starry and silent as this. Everyone is so weary of the war, and scared. And our lovely Charleston seems all in ruins from the shelling and the fires. The party decorations are elegant. Mother organized it all to perfection to lift everyone's spirits. I'm excited to see my friends' reactions— and the band is composed of members of The Citadel band, what few there are who aren't fighting. Mother says most of the cadets who are playing are those who were injured and returned to the school because their homes had been burned.

Dear Jeremiah. What a sweetheart he is. He is threatening to join the soldiers in defense of our city and the South. But he is no soldier. He is a poet, a dreamer, and my sweetest of hearts. Why do men, even men of a sensitive nature, dream of war while women dream of romance?

A sudden breeze fanned Sarah's hair from her face. She turned her chin to the sky to feel the light wind on her neck. The book rested against her chest as she imagined the party and Charlotte's excitement over the coming celebration. So Jeremiah was Charlotte's boyfriend.

The breeze stopped and she read on.

Father says he has a special unveiling tonight of something he has purchased for mother. He is very agitated about it and anxious that his surprise not be spoiled. He and mother seem so close. I hope someday Jeremiah and I will share a similar life together. How fortunate we would be to have the same caring and prosperous home they have built together. But our lives will have to wait if the tales of another bombardment come true.

Father says the special gift tonight holds the key to our future. He has been very mysterious about it all.

Sarah's phone rang in the room below. She decided to ignore it, nearly changed her mind, then let it go. She would check it later. Maybe it was Jack.

She had never been big on fits of temper or emotion in front of people. She'd been horrified at her loss of composure in front of Crystal this afternoon. It was just that her disappointment was so complete. She'd never been riding as high as she'd been before Rachel came in and banished her to the office. As for now, she'd read more of Charlotte's diary. She wanted to know how her party had gone…and what the surprise was her father had planned.

She knew how wrong stealing the diary was. But her compulsion to take it had turned into a compulsion to keep it—at least until she'd finished reading it. Maybe that's why she wasn't devouring it in one sitting: She knew when she was done, she would return it to Jack and this was the only link she had left with the discovery of her lifetime.

She settled into her rocker.

I'm wearing the pale green ashes dress tonight. Mother says it complements my coloring. She says people with green eyes should wear green often, that it provokes a visual drama and is appealing to men. I hope that I will be appealing to Jeremiah tonight. He is so dear and quite handsome. He will wear his new tuxedo that his father had sent from Saville Row in London. Mother says it is the newest of fashions for gentlemen. Jeremiah and I should look very much the couple. I wonder if he will bring me a flower. He so often does.

I'll wear the soft leather dancing slippers father brought me from Italy. He knows how I love to dance. I think the surprise for mother has Father very, very excited. The crate the workmen brought in this afternoon was several feet wide and tall! I am quite light-headed with excitement. Just a few hours until guests begin to arrive. I will write more after the party.

Sarah closed the diary and let herself drift off to sleep. It had been a long few days, and a quick nap would feel really great.

She woke to the sound of her phone ringing again. At first she couldn't figure out where she was or what was happening...but once she was oriented, she went downstairs and answered the phone.

Chapter 13

Jack had been slack-jaw-shocked by Rachel's treatment of Sarah. He'd seen his mother decimate people she considered underlings. He didn't like that in his mother, and he sure as hell didn't like it in Rachel—especially directed at someone as good-hearted and hardworking as Sarah.

He already missed her company, her quiet efficiency. She knew what needed to be done and he could trust her to handle the materials properly despite the lapse on the first day. He liked the way she hummed along with the radio. And the look on her face when she caught him dancing? Priceless, as the commercial would say. Priceless. And that tangle of hair and that delightful hills-of-North Carolina accent? Sure, he had a southern accent, too, but hers was a whole different ballgame. Almost with an Irish lilt. She was no-nonsense. Honest. He liked her straightforward attitude. As it turned out, he liked a lot about Sarah Singleton. He would call her when he got back to his room. He didn't have her phone number and he couldn't exactly ask Rachel. Sarah'd gotten his attention—she was something...really something.

Rachel had returned to the ceramics room not long after their argument. They'd been working almost hostilely since. He handed her a belt buckle with the initial B engraved on the front.

He could call Sarah's office. Maybe the secretary would be there. What was the name Rachel'd mentioned earlier? Carmen? Nahh, that wasn't it....Carrie? Chrissie....Crystal. That was it. Crystal. He looked at Rachel.

"Gotta take a whiz...be back in a minute," he said, tossing his clipboard on the table.

"Need some help," Rachel asked in her most tantalizing voice.

"No...but thanks," he said, leaving as quickly as he could without running.

He passed the nearby men's room, a little worried Rachel might follow him, and bounded up two flights of stairs to the corresponding men's room on the second floor. It was empty. The building was very quiet with most of the students out on summer break. Jack did a search on his phone for the arts department and quickly rang the number.

"Crystal Murphy," the voice said.

"Crystal, this is Jack Chase. May I speak with Sarah?" His voice echoed off the old ceramic tile walls.

"I'm sorry Mr. Chase, but Sarah's gone for the day. May I help you?"

"I really need to get in touch with her," he said smoothly while trying to sound urgent enough to inspire action from Crystal. Actually this was urgent. He did need to talk to Sarah. Now. It had suddenly become imperative.

"We don't generally give out phone numbers and addresses

Mr. Chase. I could have her call you if you like."

"I'm kind of in a hurry to speak with her…it's about the project. I need her input."

Crystal didn't speak immediately. He could almost hear her on the other end deciding whether or not to give out Sarah's number to someone she'd never met.

"She thinks you're really great—I mean, at what you do," Crystal said. "I know I shouldn't say this, but she was really upset when she left here," she said, then rattled off the number and Sarah's address.

"Thanks Crystal. I owe you."

Seconds later Sarah's phone rang and went straight to voice mail.

"This is Sarah Singleton…"

Damn.

"Sarah. This is Jack Chase. I need to talk with you. It's really important. Call me. Please. It's important."

He took a deep breath and caught his reflection in the mirror. What was he doing? *Let it go.* Finish the job and get back to the school and your safe little job. No stress. No worries.

No future. No fun. No excitement. No life.

He looked at the silent phone in his fist then at the man in the mirror.

For the first time he understood that although he and Rachel had been members of the same herd they were of a different breed. They came from the same place. They had the history of childhood but that was where the similarity ended. While before he'd always been proud of his background, now he felt embarrassed. Possibly because of how he'd used his advantages poorly. Sarah had come from nowhere to be a professional person, a good person.

He felt a connection with Sarah. It was new, tenuous and unexplored, but something was there, unfamiliar and scary, but mesmerizing, drawing him in to something he didn't quite understand. He had to see where this would lead, like he'd just read the opening chapter of a really great mystery and was anxious to enjoy the rest of the journey.

He would turn the page.

But for now, work was all that really mattered. This was his chance and he still had to remember that the opportunity had come from Rachel. The last thing he wanted to do was cause Rachel to be even harder on Sarah. He just needed a little time to figure this out—and to make a success of this project. A big success. He wanted his profession back. His work had driven him since the realization during college that art and its mysteries mattered to him. Unlocking those mysteries also unlocked a passion in him that nothing else—and no one else—ever had.

Yes, he wanted that part of his life back. He had to make this work. And he had to get Rachel to back off. And Sarah.

But for now, the police station. Needed to get the statement out of the way.

Chapter 14

*D*addy…" Sarah said, more surprised than she could ever remember being in her life.

"Hello, daughter. Hope you are doing well."

"I'm fine."

"You sure did look prosperous at your grandmother's funeral, girl."

"That was almost five years ago." Her voice sounded cold to her, her chest was tight. *What did he want?*

"And I hope you had a happy birthday this year."

Her mind immediately went to her 12th birthday. Her father had come home with a wrapped package. She couldn't believe it…he never bought anyone presents. When she went to him and thanked him, excited as only a 12-year-old girl can be, he looked at her with disdain.

"This ain't for you girl. Your brother's getting his Eagle Scout badge tonight—deserves a nice gift for that achievement."

That was the last time she had ever expected anything from

him…and she realized now, any man.

"How old are you now, girl?" he said, dragging her back to the here and now.

"How are the boys?" she asked, "Is everyone well?" *Why was he calling?*

"Yep. Everybody's health is doing just fine. But girl we have a little problem up here."

She had to force herself to ask.

"What do you need?"

"Hard times and all. The economy."

She realized where the conversation was headed.

"I was wondering if you could spare a little to help out the family. It's a tax situation…might lose the farm."

She could hardly breathe and was unable to respond.

"We need a little to keep the tax man off our backs.

"How much?" she heard a voice far away asking.

Chapter 15

Jack sat restlessly at a desk in the squad room of the Charleston PD. The building itself didn't say Charleston—more of a 1960s no-style kind of building. It did, however, look out onto Lockwood Avenue and Brittlebank Park and the Ashley River beyond. The inside of the building was as nondescript as the exterior and could have been any room, anywhere.

Mallory had seated him here at this desk and asked him to start writing down what he remembered about finding the body. He could see Mallory in his office with a distraught older couple. Officer Owens stood nearby and he went over to her.

"Officer Owens?"

"Yes…oh hi. Abby…call me Abby. I remember you from the murder scene."

"I was wondering…are those the parents?" he nodded toward Mallory's office.

Owens winced and nodded yes. "They were out on their

boat, got the message from the Coast Guard. Just got here."

Jack returned to the desk and was just finishing up when the couple stood to leave the office and a young woman approached from the hallway. The couple and the young woman fell into each other's arms in sobs.

"They think drugs…" he caught snips of the conversation. "No. Not Craig. I kno…"

Officer Owens came to him. "Are you finished?" she asked, a more official tone taking over from the earlier casual conversation.

"Yeah." He handed her the paper.

"Det. Mallory wants to speak to you before you go."

She escorted him to the now empty office, past the grieving trio.

"Mr. Chase," Mallory stood to meet him at the door. "I have a request from the family and the girlfriend. They want to meet you."

"Oh…no…I…" Jack could feel himself shrinking from the idea when Mallory motioned to the parents who suddenly were standing right in front of him. Mallory introduced them as Harold and Marsha Duncan, and Emily Randall.

"I know you found our son, called 911, stayed with him until the police arrived," the man said, extending his hand. "Not everyone would have handled it that way. Likely would have left him there. Not willing to get involved. I wanted to thank you."

Jack nodded. "I couldn't have left…I'm so sorry for what happened. Really, really sorry." He looked at each of them and his stomach clenched, their loss finding a home in his gut.

As quickly as the parents had been there, they were gone, leaving the girl behind with Skeet Mallory.

Jack went to the elevator and as he waited, he saw Mallory

and Emily Randall going through the contents of a box, may of the items in baggies. He guessed these were the contents of Craig Duncan's backpack and pockets. The girl wiped away tears, as the elevator dinged its arrival.

This suddenly had become more personal.

Chapter 16

Old houses and clutches of tourists were a blur from the back seat of the taxi as Jack left the police station and headed to see Rachel. He needed to convince her he'd leave the project in protest over Sarah's dismissal. He sure didn't want to—and maybe he wouldn't if it came right down to it.

He didn't know the answer to that one.

How could Sarah Singleton suddenly be almost as important to him as resurrecting his career? It was insane. The last thing he needed was to mess up this opportunity to get his career back. And getting involved with the woman at the center of the work was dumb, dumb, dumb. Been there, done that. Didn't plan to go there again. Never again.

Two days ago his life had been uncomplicated—and uninteresting. Now it was neither. He didn't know whether he was pissed off or elated. Probably a little of both. Maybe a lot of both. Damn.

But for now he was going into the lioness' den. He would

make Rachel see reason. The cab whizzed down King Street, past Juanita Greenberg's (he'd washed down many a quesadilla there with cold Coronas) and past the behemoth and nondescript Post and Courier building. He used to know a few folks there…probably still did.

He settled back in the seat and closed his eyes. He had to figure something out before he got to Rachel's house.

And then he knew how to do it.

"Driver. Take me back to the newspaper."

ack walked into the lobby and asked for Dan Banyon, a fraternity brother from his USC days. Dan'd been at the USC School of Journalism. He'd studied photography and landed a job at the newspaper right out of college. He'd been there ever since. Jack hadn't seen him in years.

The guard gave him the photo department number and directed him to the public in-house phone on the far wall.

Within minutes Dan was in the lobby signing Jack in and hauling him up to the second floor where they hashed over old times for the better part of an hour. Jack had forgotten how Dan filled up a room. He was a big guy, 6 feet five inches or more, with a huge personality. And smart.

"So what brings you here?" Dan asked.

Jack explained the project to him. Dan was interested and asked to see the statue and trunks. Jack knew he'd caught his attention and the result would be his way of changing Rachel's mind. By morning, the find would be news, Sarah would be a big part of that news, and Rachel would be unable to keep Sarah off the project. To do so would show her to use questionable judgment.

Jack called Sarah on his way back to the college.

"Sarah?"

"Jack."

I need you to come to the college. Now. It's important. It could change everything.

"But Rachel…"

"Just come."

Sarah arrived ten minutes later, flushed, excited.

"Hi Jack," she said as she stepped over the camera bag blocking the doorway. A portable light on a tripod was glaring down on the dresses, shoes and accessories laid out on the table. A photographer snapped away.

"Dan, this is Sarah Singleton."

Dan turned, shook hands quickly and returned to his work. Brent Baker, the reporter, began asking Sarah questions almost before she got in the door. They talked for nearly an hour. Dan shot photos of her as she examined the pieces and a short video as she explained their significance. Before the night was over, the journalists had chronicled the find and had a first-rate story for the following day's front page. And Sarah's name was interspersed throughout. The reporter was as interested in the way she found the cache as he was in what she'd found. She was inseparably tied to the project by the time the interview was over.

"Rachel will be furious," Sarah said. "She didn't want any publicity until everything was authenticated."

"Yeah, she'll go nuts." Jack said. "But publicly she won't have a choice but to praise you. There'll be no way for her to keep you out now. She's officially lost control."

Sarah tucked the small leather shoes into the case on the floor, her hair hanging in a riot of curls over her shoulder.

"I thought I told you to stay away from here," Rachel's voice sliced the moment like a shard of flying glass.

Jack and Sarah turned in unison to face their accuser.

"What the hell is going on here tonight? I got a call from Professor Johnson that a party was in progress, with strobe lights and music blaring. He was apparently right."

"Rachel. We're just cleaning up the place after the interview."

"What interview?"

"It seems the newspaper got wind of the find and came over to interview Sarah and me about it. Complete with pictures I might add. It's 1A tomorrow."

"We'll just see about that." Rachel whipped out her phone and dialed in 411. Punching in the number she glared back and forth from the phone to them. She listened intently then punched in another number. Jack recognized it for what it was—phone tree hell. She punched in more numbers and waited. Nothing. Her face was getting redder by the second. Jack glanced at Sarah. She was trying not to laugh.

"You're playing a very, very dangerous game, Jack. You have no idea."

Her tone was rigid, almost frightened. She almost had him believing there was some kind of danger.

"I guess I'll just have to go over there," she said, turned on her heel and for the second time today, stomped down the hall, her spike mules alternately slapping the stone and the bottoms of her feet as she retreated.

Sarah could hold her laughter no longer and sputtered. Jack followed suit with a high-five.

"That was spectacular," Sarah said, choking the words out

between giggle fits. "She won't be able to stop them will she?"

"Are you kidding? Dan said they'll put the photos and a bare bones story up as soon as they get back to the paper. With the main story and photos running tomorrow." But the nagging thought that Rachel was actually frightened lingered.

He pulled out his phone and pulled up the paper's website.

"And there it is!" The story brief and several photos were already posted promoting the full story in tomorrow's paper.

"Rachel will be lucky if she can even get up with anyone to vent her rage to."

Jack nodded his head imagining Rachel's frustration at not being able to get the story pulled.

"They're not giving this story up after already promoting it."

He glanced at his phone.

"What time does it go to press?" Sarah asked, looking over his shoulder at the photos.

"Brent said the first edition goes to press at ten." He glanced at his phone."

"It's 8:47. Once it's in print, it's too late."

"That fast?"

"Yep. And even if she could talk them into pulling it for the final edition, the first run would still be on the street. You can't put toothpaste back in the tube once it's squirted out. Score one for us," he said raising his hand for a high five. She obliged. It was the most hopeful she'd felt all day.

"I want to show you something," she said suddenly, taking his hand and leading him from the building to her car parked nearby. "Get in," she said, opening the car door and waving him in.

The warm night air calmed him as her hand worked the gear stick expertly, shifting from second to third as she took the ramp up to the James Island Connector. When she shifted to fourth gear, he could feel the vibration of the car, the power of the engine.

She maneuvered Folly Road to oceanfront Center Street, then headed north. Within minutes she pulled to the side of the road near a boardwalk flanked by massive granite boulders: man's attempt to stave off the erosion that storms had wrought.

"The washout. It's where all the surfers come. All the houses washed away years ago. Come on."

She hopped out of the car, opened the trunk, grabbed a blanket and met him on the other side. Motioning toward the beach she led the way up the steps to the boardwalk and onto the beach. They walked closer to the outgoing tide.

"New moon tomorrow night. Perseid meteor shower tonight. Viewing should be great," she said, flinging the blanket out. "And it's a clear night. Should be beautiful."

"It's already beautiful," he said. Another couple walked along the shoreline 50 feet away holding hands, heads bowed, deep in conversation.

He was drawn to Sarah—not in the same way he'd been drawn to Nadia. That'd been insanity from the get-go. This was all mixed up with the project and the fact that she was just so darned smart, organized…and he felt more like the man he wanted to be with her.

He wanted to kiss her.

"A meteor!" she shouted and pointed. He saw it as it neared the horizon.

"Beautiful," he whispered.

He didn't remember a lot of what Rachel had told him about Sarah, but one thing that stuck was that Sarah had left her family behind because they were poison to her. He admired her ability to separate from a family that had not been nurturing. He'd been unable to do so until disaster struck. If his family had been poor, would it have been easier? Probably, he had to admit. They'd bought and paid for him time and time again. No wonder they'd felt they owned him. No wonder he'd felt it, too.

Headlights strafed the beach then flicked off. He turned to look, but saw nothing.

"I need to know more about you." How many times had he said those words to a woman? Probably hundreds by now. But this was the first time he'd actually wanted to hear the answer. All he'd wanted in his old life was to win the prize.

She smiled up at him and his heart raced again.

His animal instinct of lurking danger went into overdrive—or had his own personal fear of getting lost inside another woman kicked in. Either way, something was scaring the hell out of him.

"What's wrong?" she asked.

He looked behind them, toward the road, and there on the steps stood someone, a man, illuminated by a streetlamp, looking in their direction.

"There's a man on the steps watching us. I'm sure of it." The man had blond hair that glowed in the full moon. He appeared to be watching them. Jack was pretty darned sure he wasn't there to watch the meteor shower.

"And there's someone with him," he whispered. She started to turn to look and he stopped her.

"This doesn't feel right. Let's go," he said, pulling himself up from the blanket and reaching down to help her stand. A medallion swung loose from his shirt and dangled there before he reached and tucked it back in just as the wind gusted and blew much of the sand from the blanket into the night air. When he looked again, the men were gone.

"I don't see anyone," Sarah said.

"They're leaving," Jack said as headlights flicked on, beamed toward the beach, turned and disappeared. He recognized it as an old Citroen, an unusual car in this part of the world.

Why would anyone be watching them? He wasn't a paranoid man—maybe the real fear was of getting involved with Sarah.

Hell, he'd actually set up situations before to seduce women while his frat brothers watched, so it's not like he was shy. He couldn't be more ashamed of many of the things he'd done in college.

But just now, on the beach, something felt bad wrong. Instinct told him the men *were* watching them.

As they retraced their drive back toward the connector bridge, he remembered seeing the car earlier, parked on the street where they made the turn toward the beach onto Center Street. He noticed it because he had a roommate once who had a car like it. The men had followed them. He was sure of it. He would come back tomorrow.

As the elevation of the road lifted, his nerves calmed and his heart rose. He watched Sarah, her hair flying in chaos around her head, as she took charge of the car and drove them off the island.

He had a random, fleeting memory of asking his mother once how he would know when he found the right person. Her answer at the time seemed inadequate and evasive. He'd resented her for not being more helpful. But now her words rang true.

"You'll just know."

Chapter 18

Jack was silent on the ride back to The Mills House.

"Breakfast. Here. Eight o'clock?" he asked as she stopped in front of the hotel.

She nodded "yes."

"See you tomorrow then," he said, unfolding his six-foot two-inch frame to crawl out of the low seat.

As he walked toward the hotel entrance, he turned around in mid-stride and waved back at her. She returned the wave as she pulled away into the night air and drove straight home. She was tired and exhilarated, so wound up she wasn't at all sure she'd be able to sleep. Had someone really been watching them on the beach? She hadn't seen anyone in the brief glance she'd gotten before he stopped her from looking. Or maybe Jack was uncomfortable being out there on the beach with her—had he taken her motives wrong?

Was that her insecurity speaking in her ear, or her good common sense warning her?

She climbed the stairs to her apartment, still mulling over

the evening's events and ready to crawl into her bed.

She slipped her key into the lock. When a shadow fell across the doorknob, Sarah froze.

Chapter 19

Morning brought fresh memories of meteors arching across black sky, waves crashing, of Sarah's amazing hair and…Jack glanced at his watch: 7:30. He'd taken a table with a view to the street so he would see her arrive. Sarah crowded into his mind. Yesterday's flashbacks to Nadia had unnerved him. Was his attraction to Sarah nothing more than a reminiscence of what he'd felt for the Russian con artist? That liaison had nearly destroyed him—in fact *had* destroyed who he used to be. But that wasn't all bad either. He hadn't exactly been Mr. Wonderful back then. The way he saw it now, he deserved what happened. But he needed to be careful. He knew his weaknesses. But most of all he still had the painful memory of what happens when demons are not kept properly caged.

Rachel was a mistake in the making if he wasn't careful.

He had to keep her at arm's length. But getting involved with Sarah was a whole different situation. Sarah wanted the statue to be authentic, and here he was again, wanting to make it happen for Sarah just as he had for Nadia. He had to keep some distance to be absolutely sure he was judging the piece on its own merits and not on what it would do for his career and for Sarah's.

Would he have kissed her last night on the beach? Probably. Would she have let him? He had no idea.

Who and why were the men watching them?

The waiter asked if he wanted coffee and soon returned with a sterling silver pot from which he poured, carefully holding a linen napkin just below the spout to catch any drips. That silver pot had probably been used to pour coffee for hung-over guests since the 1800s. Another server deposited a linen napkin-clad basket of hot biscuits.

"I'm expecting someone. I'll wait to order," he said. "Do you have this morning's paper?" The aroma of the biscuits caused him to salivate.

"I'll get a copy for you, sir." The waiter retreated with his coffee pot and returned with The Post and Courier.

Jack unfolded the paper and there was the story. Sarah's smiling face beamed on the front as she showed off the delicate leather slippers they'd found in the trunk. He smiled back at the 1A photo. Sarah was something. He checked the door. Not yet. He began reading the story. About halfway down the first column, a hand crashed down through the top of the newspaper. Jack looked up to see Rachel glaring down at him.

"I don't appreciate you going behind my back to grab publicity, Jack. There was a time when you had more class than that.

"Rach…"

"You're picking up some bad habits from the company you're keeping." She plopped herself in the chair opposite him.

"If you're referring to yourself, then you'd be right. If you mean Sarah, then you'd be dead wrong."

He folded the newspaper, picked up a roll and slathered it with butter.

"She's got more class than the two of us put together," he said, locked eyes with her and took a big bite.

"You need to leave her alone. She's done nothing to you—so back off."

"She's trying to come between us and I don't appreciate it one little bit."

"There's no us for her to come between."

"We have history, Jack. We can make a lot more. You felt it Tuesday even if you did put me off."

He hadn't taken Rachel as seriously as the present circumstance indicated he should have. Thwarting her efforts to seduce him his first day back in Charleston was the smartest thing he'd done so far. He was excited about being back in Charleston and Rachel was a familiar part of his past—a deadly combination that could have spelled disaster.

"You need to be aware I had a call from Dirk Atkinson this morning. He's demanding I inquire into the project with the possibility that it be closed down."

"Why?" Jack nearly choked on the last bite of roll.

"Now," Rachel said, pulling out a chair and sitting down. She leaned forward, locked her eyes on Jack's and said, "You listen to me. He's not at all amused about the publicity in this morning's paper. He feels it casts a bad light on him. This is a big job for his contracting company. He wants to see Sarah. Right away."

"This doesn't involve Atkinson. He's not even part of the

college. For crying out loud, Rachel."

"Everything that touches the renovation involves him. You're not that naïve. And if you're waiting for your girlfriend...."

"She's not my girlfriend. I hardly know the woman." Jack's face was hot and his anger rose to a boil.

"Like I said, if you're waiting for your girlfriend, I don't think she'll be showing up for your little brunch.

"What have you done?"

She and I had a little chat last night after she returned from her "date" with you.."

"It wasn't a date. And if you've done something to her..." he was cut off by Rachel's finger tracing the side of his face, the hint of perfume floating over the aroma of fresh bread.

"Nothing you shouldn't have done yourself," she said. He swatted her hand away.

"Meaning what?"

"Meaning I filled her in on our relationship—our ongoing relationship."

"Rachel, listen, I told you yesterday, it's been over between us for nearly a decade. We're friends. That's all. Since when did you get so serious?"

"Well, regardless, she saw it my way. She was particularly surprised to hear we were once engaged."

Jack's stomach turned.

"What did you say to her?" he asked, standing up and tossing his napkin in his seat, searching his wallet for cash. He threw a ten-dollar bill on the table. "Well?"

"I told her we'd been about to marry and we'd always had an understanding we'd be a couple again someday.

He'd just been wondering if he needed distance from Sarah—but not permanent distance.

"I told her all about the games we used to play with people of her ilk.

Jack felt the blood drain from his face.

"You remember, Jack, when we'd bet on whether you could bed some hick, and how fast. You were the master at talking the panties off the country-come-to-town set.

"Oh my God. Rachel." He felt sick.

"You considered it part of their education—kind of an adjunct professor role.

"What the hell is wrong with you Rachel?"

"Oh—and she thinks we made mad passionate love your first night in town."

"You're sick. Why would you do something like that? I told you. I don't feel the same way you do. And we didn't make love—mad, passionate or otherwise."

"Don't tell me that bumpkin has wormed her way into…"

"You're disgusting," Jack said, nearly knocking the chair over as he exited the hotel restaurant.

Chapter 20

J ack flagged a cab sitting across the street and gave the
driver Sarah's address.

Her car was in the driveway when he arrived.
Good. He paid the cabbie, asked him to wait then took the
inside steps two at a time. His knock went unanswered.
Another knock. Nothing. She had mentioned a widow's walk
in passing.

He went back outside and looked up to the roof. A wisp
of dark curl blew in the breeze from the widow's walk.

"Sarah!" he called to her. She peered over the railing then
disappeared from view. "Sarah!" Nothing. He ran up the
stairs and rapped on her door again. He was about to knock
again when the door opened. He nearly hit her in the head
with his knuckles.

"Geez, Sarah."

"What do you want?"

"I just want you to know that I have great respect for you."

"What did you say to Rachel to make her think we had

something going on with each other? Our relationship is strictly professional."

"And I know that. Rachel thinks that if I don't want her, then there has to be some reason other than herself. So you are the reason she has decided on," Jack said as forthrightly as he could.

"I'm having trouble even thinking of her as a friend. No friend would do this to someone they care about."

"Do what, Jack? Win a bet? How could you play such despicable games? What a horrible man. I have no desire to work with you…or her anymore."

"That's not me. Not now. That was before."

"Jack, I am not a stupid woman. You're good-looking, rich, smart. But there seems to be one real important link missing in your chain, mister. Character."

Jack was stunned and had no way to argue back. She was right. Who was he really? He'd spent his life not giving a damn about other people, and then, the first time he got burned himself, he ran away, retreated from the game. This was his first trip back into the world of the living and it wasn't going too great. He could turn and run, retreat back to his boring life, or stand his ground this time and fight.

"We have work to do. I'm not interested in your personal life…or Rachel's."

She was at least willing to work on the project with him.

Chapter 21

The ride to the college had been frosty, but once there, the work chipped away at the chill between them. Within minutes they were taking notes and making light comments about the growing catalogue of artifacts.

He watched her handle each piece with care, visibly enjoying the feel of the different textures. She turned suddenly and caught him staring.

"Get to work, mister."

By noon, they'd finished listing of all the contents. And he was starving. He'd missed breakfast, and he liked his three squares a day.

"How about a little lunch?" he said, a little tentatively.

"It seems I have a command meeting with Atkinson," she said coolly. "And we're done here for the morning. We can meet back here after my meeting."

He didn't answer. He was embarrassed by what had led to a place where she wouldn't even grab a sandwich with him.

He'd been trying to blame Rachel, but the real blame had to reside on his own shoulders where it belonged.

He'd managed to disappoint three people in one day. Sarah, Rachel and himself.

"I understand," he said finally. He took her hand and politely shook it.

With that she picked up her purse and with a toss of her spectacular auburn hair, headed down that long hallway he'd been watching women disappear into all week. The inevitable slam of the heavy old door that opened to the parking lot punctuated her departure. He watched from the window as she backed away. *And there she goes.* He stood there a full two minutes after she disappeared, rethinking the last few days. He had to make Rachel back off. He also had to make her see that for her not to do so would be the end of any chance they'd ever have of even being friends.

But Rachel…her reactions were way out of proportion to what was going on. And there still seemed to him an undercurrent of fear associated with Rachel's actions. Something wasn't adding up.

He was pulled from all that heavy thinking by the sound of the door opening again and footsteps returning.

He turned to the door, his heart racing with anticipation of her return. "Sar…" he said, putting a halt to he greeting when he saw the black shoulder length hair that was Rachel's.

"I saw her leave here. Are you really that cavalier about her job?

"No. Not at all…"

"You're playing a dangerous game here Jack. And remember she doesn't have our millions to fall back on."

"You're not worried about her, Rachel. Don't pretend you are."

"Wrong, Jack. Oh, so very, very wrong. You have no idea what you're doing."

She came closer, locked her eyes on him. "Take me to lunch. We need to talk about the statue."

"You know Rachel, I don't need this." He picked up his bag and turned to leave.

"So you're going to run back to that boring old hotel?"

"No Rachel, back to West Virginia and my boring professor's life." He grabbed his notebook and stuffed it into his tote bag. "Bye Rachel. The notes Sarah and I made are over there on the table."

She stood between him and the door.

"Have at it sweetheart…I hope you're a huge success…and I mean that in the most sincere way possible."

He pushed past her and this time *his* were the footsteps that echoed down the hall, *his* the hand that forced open the creaking door. As he crunched across the gravel lot, the door slammed heavily into its lock behind him, shutting out yet another chapter in a life that really was not going at all the way he had hoped.

Chapter 22

Jack Chase could go to hell. And for that matter so could Atkinson.

The project manager questioned her motives, wanted to know what had been found so far and demanded a list of the contents of the find. He said the administration was on his back about it and that he was responsible for any damage to any important pieces.

"Every single item—do not leave anything out. And get it to me immediately."

"But…"

"You have been a nuisance about this since day one. Now get me that inventory."

She'd returned to her office, made a copy of the inventory and returned it to Atkinson's office. When she arrived, his secretary said he'd just left, that Sarah might be able to catch him.

"I'll try to catch him. What kind of car does he drive?" Sarah asked over her shoulder as she hurried for the door. If

she hurried, she might could catch him.
"Some funky old European thing."

Chapter 23

Back at her apartment, in a world where she was in charge, she thought Atkinson's behavior seemed even more outrageous than it did at the college. Was that his car last night at the beach? She had not caught sight of him as she left his office. She rubbed her arms to dispel the chill creeping over her skin despite the heat of the day.

She picked up the newspaper from the coffee table to reveal the diary hiding beneath. How careless. She shouldn't have left it lying around like that, but when you live alone, what difference does it make? She looked at her picture in the newspaper. It reflected yesterday's face, the one that beamed as she showed the cameraman the leather slippers. As she read the caption her eyes began to burn and fill.

She picked up the diary, lifted her glass of pinot noir and headed up the stairs. Snagging her Nikon binoculars she ascended the steps to the widow's walk. She'd spend some time watching for dolphins and try to enjoy the afternoon. It's not like she didn't have a life. A happy life. It would be nice to have someone to share it with, but she was far from needing anyone else to make her existence count for something.

The breeze bordered on cool, with humidity no where near the ninety percent it'd been earlier in the week. She slipped into the double-seated white glider swing and lifted the binoculars to survey the harbor. The "Pride of Charleston" was out on its every-other-hour tourist cruise under full sail. It was always a beautiful sight making its daily jaunts from the Maritime Center, around Fort Sumter and to The Battery. The antebellum mansions stood regally to greet those from "off"—as the tourists were known to the locals—and waited ready to withstand the next "unpleasantness" be it hurricane, war or even the tourists themselves.

She considered it a privilege to live in a city so charming, so steeped in history, so fortunate to have this harbor and people who cared enough to make the most of all of the elements that she was enjoying right this minute.

She settled into the chair and closed her eyes to the sunshine and the soft ocean breeze that made the heat bearable.

Rachel had been vicious, listing more than two-dozen women she personally knew Jack'd been with. It'd gone on and on. Sarah had felt embarrassed for Jack. At some point in the middle of the tirade, Rachel picked up the newspaper and waved it around as evidence that Sarah was a headline-grabbing ingrate. A corner of the diary had been exposed, but Rachel had given no indication she'd seen it. It was almost as if there was something else going on that Sarah was unaware of. The tirade was out of proportion to the situation—even for Rachel.

Sarah opened the book and began to read again.

The party was as beautiful as I had dreamed. Jeremiah and I walked into the garden and he boldly took my hand. The band—

really just four injured cadets soldiering on— played a Strauss waltz. The music filled the garden and Jeremiah took me in his arms and whirled me around the flagstone walkway. The walkway is special to mother. Father had the workmen lay it around the fountain. "Mother's fountain," we call it because Father had it built just for her. She has a small table and two chairs placed near it on the west side so when the east wind blows the spray drifts in that direction. It cools her as she sits by it in the afternoon when it is particularly warm. I love to sit with her and we talk about our friends and what new dresses we will make from the materials Father brings back with him from his trips. We do not talk of war and dying. We have an understanding between us that it is forbidden when we sit by the fountain. The men speak of it so often, our fountain conversations, as we call them, are a respite from the unpleasantness that constantly threatens us and the men we and our women friends love. I wish this would all end before it gets worse, but I fear it will not.

But the party. Jeremiah and I danced and the music drifted and the sweet scent of gardenias hung in the air, and I imagined all was right with our world and we would forever be safe and dancing through our very pleasant lives.

A soft easterly wind blew across the widow's walk, the same breeze Charlotte and her mother had enjoyed. She was drawn back to Folly Beach and Jack. She put the binoculars down and drew a ragged breath as she watched the sunshine flashing on the choppy waves. The scene blurred and she wiped her cheek. It was too late to back away unscathed. She'd trusted in her judgment of him. Only the creepy man watching them had saved her from a big mistake.

Had Charlotte ever known such disappointment, or had she lived in a time when men could be counted on to be exactly what they appeared to be? She read forward several more pages before coming on a passage that seemed important.

Jeremiah has decided to join his father as he enlists in the Army of the Confederacy. My heart will surely break if he leaves. We had a future of such promise and hope. I at first begged him to reconsider. His father is a man of great strength and is an outdoorsman. He has been running supplies to the troops.

Jeremiah is a strong man too, but in a more studious way. He has never been the hunter his father is. Jeremiah is more adept in his studies and literature. But he is determined to do take this reckless path. He says it is a matter of honor, of doing the right thing. I think it is selfish and unnecessary. But knowing my woman's tears will not dissuade him, I will offer him my full support. I do not want him to leave with a guilty heart, worried for my state of mind. He must believe I wish only for his success and subsequent return to me and our life.

Sarah lifted the binoculars once more and looked into the harbor toward Fort Sumter on its lonely island. She recalled photographs she'd seen of the destroyed fort following the relentless bombardment by the union troops.

Her mobile dinged on the side table. A text message. Jack. She read the message without picking up the phone.

"Resigned from the project. Can't work with Rachel. Leaving Charleston tomorrow. Should never have come."

She put the binoculars on the side table, sipped her pinot and looked away from the mobile.

Should she respond. Obviously he wanted her to or he would've just flown away without a word.

She left the widow's walk, climbed down the steps into the apartment and thought for a few seconds. She spied the newspaper lying on the couch, the diary peeking out from underneath. She retrieved it, flipped carefully through several pages and decided to hide it in plain sight among the many books on her bookshelf. She removed the jacket from King's Pet Sematary and wrapped it onto the diary. It was a little big, but a good camouflage.

"You're leaving?" she finally texted back.

This was not what she'd hoped for. He was definitely what the project needed. Of that she had absolutely no doubt. His dedication was real and his expertise remarkable. If she couldn't be working on it, at least if he was there she would have faith that it would be taken care of properly. She'd been spellbound by his insights, his methodology. And she knew that he would succeed in identifying the statue and would resolve the issue of its worth.

"The project needs you." She looked at the words for a few seconds before hitting "send."

The response was immediate. "If I stay, it will be for one reason only."

Chapter 24

Floating through Sarah's fading consciousness, as she drifted between awake and asleep, was the diary. She'd not told Jack about it yet. What would have been simple to accomplish had now become nearly impossible to achieve. How could she possibly have anticipated the twist events had taken today? How could she have anticipated being thrown off the project? Would she still have taken it had she known? Something inside her said she might have, probably would have. The bond between her and Charlotte Beaufain seemed to grow with every page she read. How could she feel this much kinship with a woman she'd never heard of until two days ago?

The diary. When Rachel showed up here this morning to tell her about Jack's past with women, had she seen the diary lying there on the coffee table? But she'd have said something if she'd noticed it. But she had never seen it, or even knew that it existed, so would not have recognized what it was. Rachel wasn't good at self-restraint. After all, no one else even knew there was a diary.

Sarah drifted in and out of sleep, in a twilight of consciousness, random thoughts flowing freely through her mind.

She and Jack had texted plans to meet in the morning at Waterfront Park near the pineapple fountain. She'd return the diary, tell him what she'd done. That she'd pilfered, stolen, the diary that first evening. If he understood, fine. If he didn't, well she'd had the opportunity to work with a world class art detective.

Sure they were both off the project officially, but unofficially, they both had enough interest vested in the find to gather clues to the statue's origin...and how the dance turned out for Charlotte Beaufain. And they both had futures that hung on the outcome of their research, official or not. She had to keep her eye on that. She knew they would see it through as far as they could.

As sleep overtook her, a noise shook her mind from the diary. Unfamiliar sounds dragged her to the surface. Her heart pounded as awareness broke through the cloud of sleep and she sat up in bed. She slipped from the covers and crept to the bedroom door. She stood completely still and looked into the living room to see a sliver of light from the outside stairwell disappear as the door to her apartment silently closed.

Chapter 25

*S*arah's text pinged on Jack's iPhone.

"Someone broke into my apartment."

He'd been groggy when he first looked at it, then reality kicked in and he was suddenly awake. Heart-poundingly awake.

"R U ok?" he texted back.

He looked around his hotel room lighted only by a street light. He sat up in bed and hit call on his mobile.

Sarah answered without preamble, "I heard a noise. I got up and looked just as whoever it was closed the door. I SAW IT JACK."

He flipped on the lamp next to the bed.

"Sarah, be sure your door is locked. Check it now," he said, not even saying hello.

"Okay," she said, and picked up the flowered umbrella resting against the wall next to the front door. Holding it by the pointed end, she angled the heavy curved handle ready to thrash any intruder she might come across as she unlocked the door and went into the hall. The door was still locked?

No one. She saw no one. She walked to the head of the lighted stairwell. Nothing. She stood there motionless for a full minute, listening for any telltale sign that someone was still there, waiting.

She finally closed the door, relocked it—for all the good that had been—and turned back to the empty living room.

She could hear Jack calling to her through the phone.

"Sarah?! Say something?!"

"I'm here. The door was locked. But I know what I saw, Jack. And I wasn't asleep. I was standing right there. Whoever it was made a noise that woke me up. I saw the door close and heard the lock click."

"I'm calling the police."

"Jack. No. There's no one here."

"Then we need to figure out who it was. Does anyone have a key to your apartment?"

Sarah's eyes widened.

"Oh, Jack. Oh, no."

"What?" he asked impatiently.

"Only two people. Mrs. Brantley. My landlady. And..."

she spat out the name:

"Rachel."

He showed up ten minutes later, sent her straight to bed, and took up residence on her sofa.

Sarah slept restlessly, but sleep for him had been a lost cause. Would Rachel really break into Sarah's apartment? And what for? Would she try to hurt her? His skin crawled at the thought of Rachel standing there in the dark watching Sarah as she slept. Something was going on with Rachel that didn't add up.

When dawn broke, he breathed a sigh of relief and allowed

himself to drift off. But even then, he slept a fitful sleep with the ever-present feeling of eyes in the dark watching.

Chapter 26

Breakfast was delicious. Sarah'd prepared one of his favorites, shrimp and grits, her secret recipe, she said. But the delicious food couldn't hide his unease with the events of the night before.

He'd actually taken a bike from in front of the hotel, figuring it would be the fastest way to get to Sarah's apartment.

"So what's your secret?" he asked, wanting to know her secret grits recipe. She looked at him blankly, then blushed.

"Hmmm. So you do have a secret. But for now, I'll settle for the secret to your grits."

He listened as she explained about stone ground grits she picked up at the Piggly Wiggly, the only place in town that carried them. They were milled just 30 miles up the road in St. George, home of the World Grits Festival. She discovered them the first year she was in town when she and some friends attended the festival. Jack scraped his plate for the last little bit and leaned back in his chair a satisfied man. He was even more intrigued with her now that he guessed she had a good little secret. He leaned forward and said. "Your grits are amazing."

"Thanks."

He looked around, not really having had time to assess her place last night. His eyes scanned the room, then turned to her.

"This is a great apartment."

She felt the heat rising in her face. "Certainly not what you're used to," she said, "But it's home to me."

"Where's the staircase go?"

"I'll show you." She led the way to the roof.

"Wow, this is awesome," Jack said admiringly. "What a view," his words were almost a whisper. "You must have the best apartment in the city."

"Not the best. But good enough." She was pleased at his sincere compliment.

"I bet you spend lots of time up here. I know I would."

"Every day unless it's storming. Even then I can watch the harbor from my living room or studio."

"You have a studio?" he walked around the rooftop porch, taking in the view of the harbor from different vantage points.

She nodded yes, and realized she was smiling, happy he understood how special her home was. When she looked back at him, he was watching her. For a couple of seconds their eyes held and her heart raced. She needed to give him the diary, but now she realized she couldn't.

She walked to a rose bush she planted in a large pot on one end of the walk and picked a yellow rose in full bloom, one of the few that had not baked in the sun.

"I'd better get this in water," she said going back downstairs.

Jack followed her, shut the door to the roof behind her and joined her in the kitchen. She filled a tiny vase and went to set it on a round table next to the couch, a flea market find, she explained, from her first year in Charleston. It was painted red and had stenciled flowers on the legs. He knew she had painted it without asking.

Her anxiety became obvious when she dropped the vase, shattering the glass on the hardwood floor. He went to clean it up.

"Stop it! I'll do it myself." She knelt to pick up the pieces.

"Sarah, it's okay."

She looked up at him with a pensive, concerned look he would do anything to dispel. He realized she wasn't used to having other people in her space both invited or otherwise.

"Sorry…" she said, dumping the glass shards into the recycle bin a dropping the rose into a juice glass of water.

But they had work to do. He told her he wanted to go back to the beach to investigate the car that had followed them. He thought he'd seen it parked at a motel near the pier.

"I'm going to shower," she said, "And then we'll go to the beach." He put the dishes in the sink and started washing them. Since he'd been on his own in his less affluent lifestyle, he'd learned to take care of himself and his surroundings. But it'd been learned behavior all the way. It wasn't something that came naturally to a guy who'd grown up with maids and butlers and yardmen doing all the humdrum daily upkeep. In the last few years he'd purposely adopted a more mainstream lifestyle and had grown to enjoy the ordinary part of his life. It gave him a feeling of control over something at a time when it was all he *could* control. But he was still somewhat of a mess. A real mess actually.

He finished the last dish and the phone rang. He didn't answer, but when the machine kicked in, an older male voice began a message, "This is for Sarah Singleton or Jack Chase." Jack picked up the phone. Who would think to call him here, except Rachel. And this certainly wasn't Rachel.

"This is Jack Chase," he said abruptly cutting off the voice that was in the process of leaving a message.

"Mr. Chase, I saw the story in yesterday's newspaper about the items found at the college. I'm a collector interested in purchasing the diary."

"Diary? I don't recall that there was a diary," Jack said. "There were several household ledgers and a novel, but no diary. Besides, the artifacts are not for sale—at least not at this time. Why did you think there was a diary?"

"Because I have the second volume. And it refers to the first book being hidden somewhere at the college."

"I see," Jack said. "Sorry. No diary. And what was your name again?" The phone clicked off. Whoever it was must have realized he'd made a mistake.

Sarah was splashing in the shower. He walked to the closed door and knocked lightly.

"Sarah?" he called out over the sound of the splashing water.

"Who's there?" she asked teasing.

"Just who are the possibilities?" he asked in mock outrage.

"Very funny," she called out. The scent of citrus shampoo seeped from under the door.

"I just had an interesting phone call. Someone asking about a diary."

The water shut off immediately.

"A diary?"

Chapter 27

The drive to Folly Beach had been easy, without the usual traffic tie-ups. The beach was a perfect blend of softly folding waves, fluffy clouds, strikingly blue sky and a refreshingly dry sea breeze.

"Tell me about the telephone call," she said as they walked out on the Folly Beach Pier. She'd put off hearing about the inquiry into the diary until they got to the beach. She knew she would have to tell him she had it once the conversation started. "Who was it?"

"He didn't give his name. He said he wanted to buy the diary that was found among the artifacts."

She believed no one knew about the diary but her. In fact she didn't see how it was possible for anyone else to know it existed.

"I told him he was mistaken, that all we'd found were a few household ledgers and a novel. I think I'd remember a diary. That would have been the most helpful, important thing we could find."

She was speechless. She needed to tell him she had the diary.

"What made him think there was a diary?" she finally asked, forcing herself to sound uninterested, clinical.

"He said he had the second volume and it mentioned the first diary being hidden at the college with the things the family left behind."

She had to tell him. Now.

"Jack," she said. They'd reached the end of the massive pier. She leaned forward on the railing, watching the slowly rolling ocean. How angry would he be when she told him, but she'd already waited too long.

"Jack."

He squinted at her. "What?"

A crack of thunder startled both of them. A cloud had blown up behind them, hidden until the last minute by the hotel near the end of the pier. A streak of lightening heralded the storm's march toward the beach. The smell of rain and another rumble caused Sarah to look toward the dunes. A man in black pants and a white dress shirt stood in front of an old European-looking car. The ash gray cloud was like a stage curtain behind him, making his white shirt stand out even more. Was there someone sitting in the car? She couldn't be sure. The smell of rain on asphalt obliterated the ocean air.

"Jack," she said, grabbing his arm. "Is that the man you saw watching us last night? The car?" When they turned to look, the man was gone from sight and the car was backing away.

"What'd he look like?"

Sarah described the small man as 60-ish with a white shirt and thinning hair.

"It's got to be the same man. Was there someone with him?"

"I think so. "I think someone was in the driver's seat. Blond, I think. I'm not sure though."

Chapter 28

By the time they got to the pier entrance, the car was long gone and rain had begun to fall. The smell of rain on hot asphalt filled the air. They ducked into Locklear's restaurant, located on the pier near the steps to the parking lot.

The aroma of fresh fish frying greeted them.

"I'm starved," she said.

"We'll have lunch," His jaw was clinched and there was a crease between his eyes.

"It sounds great," she said, but the man was still on her mind. Had she seen him somewhere before? She shook it off. There were other things to think about than some creepy man in a funky old car.

"I have to think the phone call about the diary and these guys following us are related," Jack said, popping a hot hushpuppy into his mouth.

She'd tell Jack about the diary when they got back to the apartment. Then she could show it to him. If he didn't freak out that she stole it, maybe they could continue the work together. She wasn't ready to give up yet.

If he did freak, she'd have no choice but to relinquish it to him so he could return it to the school. He might be so furious he would just take it and leave. Turn her in to Rachel, the police even, have her fired and that would be that. No job, no nothing. All because of an impulsive moment she still couldn't explain or even justify to herself. Temporary insanity. That was the only reason she could imagine.

Chapter 29

The bottle of Chardonnay was cold and sweet with the crabmeat stuffed flounder and chilled, peppery coleslaw.

"Fantastic," he said, leaning back in his chair, much like he had after breakfast this morning. It was fun watching him eat. The boy liked his groceries.

Dishes rattled as a waitress cleared the table next to them. The pier-side restaurant was busy.

"What's so funny?" he asked, his eyes crinkling at the corners in merriment.

"You."

"Me?"

"You're quite a guy, Mr. Chase."

"And you're quite a gal, Ms. Singleton."

His mobile rang.

"This is Jack," he answered and listened intently. "Any other surprises, Ben?" He nodded his head as if in agreement with the caller. "Send the report to the Mills House—I'm staying there."

"We have at least one answer," he said, a big grin spreading across his face.

He held his glass up in a salute to her.

She lifted hers and their glasses clinked.

"That was the lab. Remember the samples I took the first day?"

"Yeah?" She looked at him, eyebrows raised in anticipation of what he would tell her.

"Traces of gold and emerald."

"Gold and…"

"You heard me. That's why this head is so important. And at least one other person already knows what's inside it. Something they're willing to kill for."

A man coming toward her locked his eyes on hers as he passed the table.

"Jack," she said, her eyes watching the man as he exited the restaurant and walked out onto the pier and the waiting blond. Jack followed her gaze. He grabbed her hand protectively.

"Do you know him?" he asked.

"I felt like he was watching me."

Music sounded from the pier and Sarah turned to look through the glass door the man had just exited.

A band on the end of the long pier was tuning up their instruments.

"Can I get you anything else," the waitress said, slipping the check onto the table.

"Live music?" Jack asked, as he pulled Sarah from her chair.

"Sweetie, we have music most every night in the summer. Beach music. People come from all over to dance on the Folly pier."

"Open to the public, I assume."

"Yessir, good-lookin', you betcha." The waitress winked at him. "Looks like the rain cloud has passed. A good night out there."

Jack paid the check, left a generous tip, and led the way to the end of the pier. The band was already into "Stand by Me" by the time they joined the gathering crowd. Some dancers were already doing their own signature moves of the shag. It was a half step more than the swing, and for those not born to it, the dance was a half-step more difficult than it looked.

Jack scouted the crowd for the man, took Sarah's hand and pulled her into the small clutch of dancers, twirled her under his arm, and broke into a big grin when he saw her body pick up the rhythm like a veteran. They held their own with the other dancers and twirled into each other's arms as the song ended.

"You do a great little shag," he said admiringly while watching the other dancers for any signs of the man. The dance was one of the first things Sarah'd learned at the College of Charleston. Her roommate had been born and raised in Myrtle Beach, the birthplace of the dance that was meant to be done with sand between the toes, on the beach or on a pier or, before it was torn down, at the Pavilion on the main drag at Myrtle Beach. And it was real obvious he'd bent an ankle many a time to the steady rhythm of beach music.

"You're perfect, aren't you?" Jack said, making her blush. He wouldn't think she was so perfect when she told him about the diary. She would tell him now. It had gone way too far.

"Jack. There's something I need to tell you."

"Okay. What?" he said.

The strange man from the restaurant was suddenly in front of them.

"Excuse me," he said, clearing his throat. "Ms. Singleton?

Mr. Chase?"

"Yes," Sarah said tentatively.

Jack echoed her "yes," eyeing the man sharply and stepping slightly in front of Sarah in a protective stance.

"Mr. Chase, we spoke this morning. I saw the article in yesterday's newspaper. I am convinced there's a diary among the items you discovered."

"As I told you on the phone, Mr.?"

"Holt. Eldon Holt. Dr. Eldon Holt. I collect Civil War memorabilia. I own a companion diary to the one you found."

"Mr. Holt, as I said, there is no diary…"

"I will pay you top dollar for the book."

"Mr. Holt, you need to leave us alone. And how did you find us here anyway? Did you follow us?"

"I have to confess I did. But I assure you I simply wish to purchase the book. If someone else has already acquired it, just tell me who…"

Jack towered over the older man.

"There is no diary, and we do not wish to be bothered further." Sarah had heard that tone of voice before—from Rachel when she was ordering people around. Jack knew how to get rid of folks he considered a nuisance or inferior. On Rachel it was irritating. But right now, in this situation, it was a comfort to be with someone who knew how to handle an interloper.

"I'll be in touch," Holt said, as he turned and walked straight-backed from the restaurant.

"What the hell?" Jack said, clutching her hand protectively, and watching Holt disappear back into the restaurant. "Following us? Last night? All day? Creep!"

"Jack," she said, squeezing his hand. "I have to tell you something. It's serious. You're not going to like it."

He looked at her intently. She hated this moment. She wished she could just disappear over the side of the pier, but she couldn't. And in that instant, she could see he'd guessed what she was going to say.

"There *is* a dairy?" His eyes were wide, he was slightly bent at the waist, his hands held out to his sides, palms toward her, in disbelief.

She bit her lip and started to look away, but found the courage to hold her gaze on his eyes.

"And you have it, don't you?" he said, evenly, without anger but with a trace of wonderment.

She nodded yes, still working her lower lip, trying not to crumble. How would he ever believe now she wasn't the kind of person who went around taking things that didn't belong to her? She had a career to consider. What kind of person would hire someone who would steal artifacts with which they were entrusted? He could ruin her with this kind of information if he was of a mind to do so. Especially after last time.

"When? Why?" he asked. His hands were now perched on his waist.

"That first night. In the shed.

"Seriously?"

"Remember. Rachel showed up and the two of you went off looking for a handcart so we could move the stuff into the main building."

"Sarah…damn…"

"I was looking through the trunk and found a key, then found the diary in the bin of random items, started reading it and just couldn't let it go."

She was babbling on, and he was watching her, obviously dumbfounded.

"It was as if I'd found something that belonged to me. I

can't explain it, Jack."

"You took it?"

"All I can say at this point is how I regret what I did. But…"

"But what?" Jack was aghast.

"I'm glad I still have it. It's our only link to the project."

He was speechless.

"I will understand if you absolutely despise me for this. I want you to know I'm usually a trustworthy person."

She was on the verge of tears.

"I don't know what came over me that night. I was going to return it," she babbled on.

"I had it in my purse to replace the night Rachel ordered me out. I never had the chance after that."

She'd never been more miserable in her entire life?

"Sarah. Come on now. Don't cry," Jack said, recovering his composure, taking her hand in his and wiping the tears that had begun to spill down her cheeks.

"Seriously, I'm kind of relieved actually."

"Re..rel…relieved?" she stuttered out the word.

"Hey, it's unsettling to be around someone who has no faults at all."

"But I stole it."

"You know you shouldn't have taken it. So do I." He pushed a stray curl of hair from her eyes.

"But the world isn't going to end because of it."

"It was wrong." Her voiced was little and shaky.

"It's not like you took it to make a buck…you weren't planning to sell it were you?"

"Of course not," she said indignantly. "I would never do something like that."

He couldn't help but smile at her outrage. But then his

skin prickled a little at the memory of Rachel's admonition not to trust Sarah too much.

"Sarah…" Jack started, then stopped. "I have to ask about something. Rachel said…"

"Oh My God…what did Rachel tell you?"

"Something about a missing miniature…that you were suspected…"

"Are you kidding me? That whole thing was about her. She picked it up to show to someone and put it in a drawer, forgot it, and when it went missing…"

"Sarah. She said she never believed you took it."

"She didn't bother to say the reason she knew that was because she mislaid it herself though, did she?"

"We're talking about Rachel here, remember. Of course it wasn't her fault."

He picked up her hand and kissed the back of it keeping his eyes locked on hers.

"I figured she wasn't too worried about you since you were still working for her."

He pushed her hair over her shoulder and kissed her forehead.

"Let's go back to your place. I want to see this diary Holt is so hot to buy."

Chapter 30

The top step squeaked ever so slightly.

The intruder stopped, listened for a few seconds and decided no one heard, or cared that someone was on the second floor. The door opened easily with the credit card trick that was always being used on the murder and mayhem TV shows.

The door clicked shut quietly and the search was on. The diary had to be here somewhere. He said the look on her face had given it all away. Jack didn't know about it, but she sure did. That was as much a fact as if she'd handed it over right on the spot.

Obvious hiding places like the dresser drawers, closet shelves, under the mattress yielded nothing. In the bathroom, a linen closet held neat stacks of towels and washcloths. She's a neat freak. Books toppled from shelves.

When the car door slammed outside, fear froze the intruder in place. They couldn't be back so soon.

Hurry. It has to be here someplace. And there on the floor, the book jacket half off…

Chapter 31

The scent of the marsh hung in the air tonight, the smell of the Lowcountry.

"Jack, it's been quite a day," Sarah said, almost whispering. "Thanks for not freaking out about the diary."

"You don't have to thank me for anything. I'm the one who needs to be doing the thanking. "Let's go inside," he said as they headed toward the porch.

Lights flashed brightly from a car that cranked on the street. As it pulled away, the glare temporarily blinded him.

He smiled as she muttered, "Tourists." Out-of-towners often parked along residential streets and walked to the battery across the street. They saw the entire town as an historic version of DisneyWorld and often failed to realize that instead of fake houses with Mickey Mouse living inside, these were people's homes and lives being invaded by strangers.

"You're cute when you get all righteous," he said, giving her a hard time.

They climbed the steps. The downstairs back door

slammed shut, startling Sarah. It was a door to the walled garden in which her landlady liked to spend her evenings. Sometimes Sarah joined her there on Sunday afternoons and they would have tea together.

"I should check on Mrs. Blanding. She doesn't usually go outside at night,"

"You want me to come with you?" Jack asked as she headed down the staircase.

"She might need some help finding the cat. Nebo gets loose sometimes and she really frets over him," Sarah called over her shoulder. "You have the keys. I'll be right back."

"I'll make us some coffee," he responded.

He knew as soon as he opened the door something wasn't right. For starters, the door wasn't locked and he remembered Sarah jiggling the handle to be sure it was latched tight before they left for the beach.

Inside, books had been pulled from shelves, papers scattered about, kitchen cabinets emptied onto the counters. Damn. What a mess. And then his heart stopped. "Sarah," he whispered then called out loud, "Sarah!"

Whoever had done this must have been leaving by the back door. That was the sound of the intruder leaving they heard as they came in the front. He took the steps down two and three at a time, nearly losing his balance, and calling, "Sarah!" the whole time. He slammed the screen door open as he passed through it into the garden. And there she was. Sarah. Lying on the ground near the wooden gate that opened onto the side street.

"SARAH! Oh my God. No, no, no. Sarah." He didn't try to lift her, but brushed the hair from her face.

"Sarah, say something. Wakeup….please wake up." He looked around him then called back toward the house… what was the landlady's name? Blanding. "Mrs. Blanding. Help! We need help out here!" The sound of his own voice carried the panic he felt inside.

He heard nothing at first, then the screen opened.

"Mrs. Blanding...call 911. Sarah's been hurt."

"Who are you?" she asked sternly.

"I'm her friend. We just came home and heard the back door slam. She thought you might need her ....and ....and ... I just found her—like this. Please. Hurry. Call 911."

He turned his attention back to Sarah, stroked her head and called to her again. "Sarah."

Within a few seconds, Mrs. Blanding joined him outside with the portable phone. She had the EMS dispatcher on the line.

"He wants to talk to you."

Sarah began to stir slightly as the dispatcher asked if she was breathing.

"Yes."

"Is there any bleeding?" the voice asked.

"No, I don't see any blood. I think she might have been hit on the head," he said. His voice was shaking.

"Sarah. This is Mrs. Blanding. Wake up, dear," the old lady said, bending from her waist and reaching down to her unconscious renter and friend.

The dispatcher said an ambulance and the police were on the way. A siren sounding in the distance grew stronger. *Please let that be for Sarah.* The siren neared and finally stopped, followed by heavy boots entering the house and coming through the hallway to the back garden.

"What's her name," the EMS technician asked.

"Sarah. Her name is Sarah," Jack said weakly.

"Sarah, you need to wake up now," the EMS worker said

firmly, ordering Sarah to wake up.

"You're safe, but you've been hurt and need to wake up," he said again.

"Has she been conscious at all?"

"She stirred a little bit at first. But not for a couple of minutes now."

As if on cue, Sarah's eyes opened. The arrival of the police added to the chaos in the tiny garden. Jack explained Sarah's apartment had been ransacked.

An officer disappeared into the house to check it out. The other stayed in the garden taking down notes as Jack described the man on the phone, and Holt who'd later approached them in the restaurant. He left out any mention of the diary. He didn't want that bit of information out there yet. It could add to the danger, knowing that a substantial treasure was the lure.

Holt was desperate to have the book. And now Jack knew why. A fortune waited for anyone who could gather all the clues to the head's location.

The EMS technicians checked Sarah out. Once she came to, she seemed to recover quickly. A goose egg had sprouted on the back of her head and a slight headache had her face pulled into a frown, but otherwise she seemed to feel okay.

She didn't want to go to the hospital, argued against it, but they insisted she go nevertheless. They did agree that Jack could drive her..

On the ride the hospital, Sarah processed all that had happened.

"I don't think whoever it was meant to hurt me—they more or less ran over me on their way out of the garden," she said, quietly.

"You could have been seriously hurt, Sarah."

"It was so dark I think they couldn't find the gate at first.

I hit my head on the edge of the chair," she said, gingerly touching the goose egg that had begun to throb.

The lights of Charleston Harbor reflected on the still water as they rounded Lockwood Drive and drove into the emergency bay at Roper Hospital.

Chapter 32

The emergency room doctor looked at Jack, then back to Sarah. We can admit her, but if you will stay with her and keep her awake for at least six hours…"

"No problem," Jack said. "If that's okay with Sarah."

She nodded her assent.

"She may have a slight concussion. So keep her awake," he looked at the clock, "until 3 a.m."

"I'll keep her awake."

"If she seems at all disoriented or the headache gets worse, bring her back in. I'd be more concerned if she didn't have that lump. Sometimes the swelling is inward instead of outward and that can be a real problem."

"I'm okay. Really. I'm fine," Sarah said, gently touching her head and wincing when she came to the point of impact. "I just want to go home and get a shower."

As Jack pulled into the driveway on East Battery he prepared her for the mess inside.

"Sarah, someone broke in while we were gone. It's a mess."

"The diary?"

Jack shrugged. "I didn't have a chance to look for it. You...I...went after you..."

Sarah got out of the car for the second time tonight and headed for the steps.

"I'll carry you."

"You'll do no such thing. I'm perfectly able to walk up a few steps." About halfway up, she stopped and waited for his arm to lean on. "Well, maybe not perfectly able."

The police officer met them as he came down the stairs.

"We're finished here for now. Until you go through your things there's no way to know what might have been taken," he said.

"Why don't you give us a call in the morning. We'll check out this Holt guy tonight. Call if you need us," he said, tipping his hat and heading out the front door.

Quiet descended.

Mrs. Blanding called up to them from the first floor, "Can I do anything, Sarah?"

"I'll be fine, really, Mrs. B."

"I've never had an intruder before. How upsetting this should happen to you. Well, goodnight, dear," she said, shaking her head and disappearing into her bedroom.

Sarah leaned on Jack as they climbed the last few steps to her door. Distress played across her face as she surveyed the chaos. Then she purposefully crossed the room to the bookshelf. After sifting through the toppled books she looked at Jack, stricken.

"I don't see it. I think the burglar took the diary. Oh, Jack. I am so, so sorry."

"Are you sure?"

"Yes, I'm quite sure I'm sorry." She smiled. "I put the diary on this shelf wrapped in the book jacket from "Pet Sematary."

"I'd never have figured you for a Stephen King freak," he said. She was full of surprises. He knelt down and sifted through the pile of books littering the floor. Just as he was about to stand, he saw the edge of the book jacket and the backwards "R" he remembered from the title of the King book. He pulled it from under the edge of the sofa.

"Sarah," he said quietly, lifting the jacket. He held it up as she turned to look.

She drew in her breath, excited.

"That's the jacket. The diary?"

"Sorry. Empty. The jacket was under the sofa. The cover hung limply as he held it up. He shook it gently. A little piece of paper fluttered to the floor.

"What's that?" she asked.

Jack bent and retrieved the paper. It appeared old, coarse.

They looked at it together. He turned it over.

"Looks like a little map. Is it yours?"

She looked at Jack, shook her head no, and took the map. She went into the kitchen, pulled a baggy from a drawer and dropped the paper into it for safekeeping.

"Maybe it fell out of the diary."

"How much of the diary did you read? Did it mention anything about a map?"

"I only read the first few pages. But," she said brightly and went to the corner of her room where her computer sat on an old schoolteacher's desk. She turned it on and the screen flickered to life. Within a minute she had opened a file and hit the print button.

"We can read it now." She handed the pages to Jack.

"What's this?"

"Look."

His puzzled look changed to excitement as he realized he held copies of the diary's pages.

"I know I said this before, but Sarah Singleton, you're a vey smart lady!" This was just the ticket to keep her awake until 3 a.m. They could spend the time reading the diary.

"It's not the whole thing. But it's a good chunk of it," Sarah said, as she surveyed the damage, shocked at the destruction of her usually ordered existence. "I didn't want to handle the pages too much so I photographed them. I'd planned to finish shooting them tonight."

"Let's not worry about all this right now," he said, comforting her with an arm around her shoulders.

"I'll make that coffee now. You curl up on the sofa and I'll be right with you. Start reading, girl."

"Yes sir," she said coyly.

By the time he returned with the coffee, she was scanning the pages she'd read the day before. She gave him a synopsis of the contents so far to bring him up to speed.

"This is the last bit of coffee," he said, handing her the steaming mug.

They read together, enjoying Charlotte's description of the party and the young gentlemen with whom she danced. But their interest was piqued by Charlotte's description of the unveiling of a piece of art her father had brought with him back from his travels in Europe. A four-foot tall statue, she said. A beautiful male form that made many of the ladies blush and hide behind their fans. A few had actually left at of the sight of it.

"Quite the scandal. My how times have changed," Jack said as Sarah began to read.

I have to admit, I was fascinated by the nude male form and was inspired to touch it. Why did I not blush like the other ladies? In fact some had been so overcome they asked their gentlemen to take them home at once. Mother smiled at their distress. She is an educated woman, unlike so many of her friends who never were allowed that opportunity. She went far away to Winthrop College where she studied art and the romance languages. She was thrilled by the present Father brought to her. I'm sure she is quite the talk of the city today, because she was unabashed in her admiration of the statue.

I had been somewhat shy in following Mother's lead in exploring the statue during the party, not being as sure of myself as she is. I was concerned of what Jeremiah would think of me should he catch me staring. What he could not know was that at the first sight of the statue, I had wondered if it was an accurate rendering of the male form. I wondered if Jeremiah would look just so—and I blushed at the thought. I could feel the heat rising into my countenance.

But later, as I stood alone in the ballroom in my nightclothes, I explored each limb, the torso and the back of the statue. And lastly I looked at the statue's male parts and imagined Jeremiah standing before me instead of this marble man. Dare I write here I reached out to touch these forbidden parts? Dare I write here in this private place the heat this provoked in me? I shall not say more, but shall go back to the statue tonight. I will once more imagine many things. I will anticipate the day when my dreams will become real.

"The first time I saw you, you were touching the statue, feeling him up," Jack said. "Just like Charlotte Beaufain going downstairs in the dead of night for her rendezvous with the statue."

"So you're a peeping Tom?" Sarah teased.

"And you're a statue molester. I was pretty upset with you for touching soft marble barehanded."

"I knew better, but couldn't help it. Charlotte's right. It's beautiful. I felt compelled to touch it—just like I was compelled to take the diary. I don't remember ever feeling connections to inanimate objects before, Jack. Don't you think it seems really strange?"

"I guess. A little. You're the one who found the piece, Sarah. You feel some ownership. It makes sense to me—so yeah, I can understand it."

"I feel a kinship with Charlotte. My hands touched what she touched. We were both called by the statue, moved by it. I have to wonder where it came from and who the artist is."

"That's something I'm determined to find out. I have a couple of calls in to experts in Italian sculpture."

"I thought you were the expert."

"Being an expert more often than not means knowing where to go for the answers," Jack said, settling deeper into the sofa.

By the time they read another couple of pages, Sarah's eyes were batting furiously to stay open.

"You can't go to sleep for another few hours. How's the headache?"

"Better...but I am very sleepy. The beach, a knock on the head and orders to stay awake aren't a great combination," she said, reaching for the coffee and taking another sip.

"Tell you what. You read to me, and I'll shelve the books. It'll give both of us something to do and keep you awake. If we sit on that couch much longer, we'll both be sound asleep."

So Sarah read and Jack straightened the mess left by—

whom? Holt? Rachel? Who else knew about it?

Most of the diary dealt with day-to-day routine, friends, possible suitors. But the tone became more and more anxious as an impending escalation of the war dampened Charlotte's high spirits.

"Father says we may have to flee the city. The war has come close. The city government and the newspaper have all moved to locations west of Calhoun Street. They say the college buildings are out of reach of the bombardment, but at night I can hear the pounding of the cannons. Robert Barre was injured yesterday when he ventured too close to The Battery. It's frightening. I heard my parents talking last night when they thought I had gone to bed. Father said he was looking for a place to store our things in case we have to leave in a hurry. He said our safety was most important. I feel safe because he is so sure we will be alive and well at the end of the war. I went downstairs last night after everyone had gone to bed. I talked to the statue. He is my confidant. When I feel lonely, he is the only one with whom I can share my feelings. I don't want anyone to know how really afraid I am of having to leave our beautiful Charleston, our loving home."

"Jack…this makes my hair stand on end. I wonder what happened to her?"

"Keep reading Sarah," he said, straightening a row of books. "You'll have to organize these the way you had them later. I'm making a mess of this."

"You're doing great," she said and continued reading. The words turned more somber as Sarah turned each page.

"We are leaving. Father says the Union soldiers are heading this way lead by a brutal General named Sherman. He has

burned Atlanta and the city surrendered last week. Many have been killed as he passed through. The news is that he has turned his troops toward the coast.

I'm frightened. Father and his foreman have been working on a hiding place for some of our worldly goods. I think it is somewhere at the college. Of course, all the students have left to be with their families both here and in other parts of the state and beyond. Some have joined the Confederate cause. The poor professors are left with empty classrooms so they too are leaving. It's a good hiding place, father says, with its many hallways and deserted rooms."

"She's talking about the hidden wall. Her father built it!"

Jack came to look over her shoulder and read the words himself.

"I cried when he told me, but I am trying to be brave. I told him how sad I was to leave the statue. He knows how attached I am to it. He says he will put it in the safe place he is building. Then he said something odd. He said that I could have the most important part of the statue to take with me."

"The head? She called it the prize. It must have contained jewels and gold...the traces the lab found." They read on for a few more pages as Charlotte wrote of her fears and feelings—all typical of a young woman. And then came the night they had to leave.

"Father came to me tonight. He brought a leather bag to show me. He told me where he planned to hide it. He says it is our family's salvation and will help us regain our lives once the war has ended. I looked in the bag and was elated and frightened

143

by what I saw. It is the important part of my dear statue—and the prize. Father had it removed so we could take it with us. He said the body would remain here, hidden, to be reclaimed after the war. It is also part of our future, he said. I do not understand how it will save our family. But father is wise and if he says it is so, then so it is."

"Jack, this is so exciting. They must have had the head when they left." He joined her on the couch. The drowsy lethargy of earlier in the evening had flown. They were both intent on finding the answers. Where did the family go?

"Father says we will leave at 3 a.m. The cannon seem louder, but I do think it has simply begun to wear on our minds. But father does seem more anxious and has arranged for our carriage to be brought around to the back of the house. We will leave by cover of darkness. I will go with him tonight to help hide the rest of the goods and this diary of our lives and flight to safety. Someday when we return, our future will be waiting for us. The small map inside this book will lead us back to the important spot. He said he would share the whole secret of the statue with me then."

He looked at Sarah, convinced the scrap of paper with the odd markings was the map Charlotte wrote about in her diary. Jack picked up the scrap of paper from the coffee table.

"The map. Jack, this has to be it." Sarah said.

They looked at it together, then back to each other. It was meaningless. It had no point of reference from which to depart. The only notation read, "Beside the Still Waters."

The script was elegant with flourishes typical of the mid- to late-1800s.

"Beside the still waters," Sarah said softly repeating the

words.

"I don't know, Jack. There's water everywhere around here, still and otherwise. We could follow water clues 'til the end of time and still never find the right starting point."

"We haven't finished reading the diary."

"I long for the day we will return and I will wear the beautiful ash green dress and soft leather slippers again. We will dance and sing. Strauss will once again bring partners together to whirl around the ballrooms in a spectacular waltz. And when this dreadful war has ended Jeremiah and I will visit this special place where I have buried our future, this place that is sacred to him and to his family, this place wherein lies our hearts still waters, to visit his past and to retrieve our future. And someday I will read these words and remember my family's bravery. I must survive. I must. But should I not, and should my dear family meet a similar fate, I ask that the Dear Lord in Heaven shelter our souls in his loving embrace."

"This seems to jump forward. Look at the dates. This is nearly two weeks after the previous entry. And Jeremiah…what of him?"

The clock chimed 3 a.m.

"We're missing a lot of information. Somehow she ended up being the one who buried the head."

Sarah yawned. "Okay doctor, as much as I'd like to keep reading, I need to sleep."

Jack kissed her forehead and nodded yes. He looked in her eyes. "Pupils are the same size," he said. "I guess you're going to make it."

"I certainly hope so."

"You sleep. I'm going to read through the first pages again. I'm not at all tired," he said.

145

She slipped deeper into the couch and stretched out her legs. Jack covered her with the crocheted afghan. Her eyes closed and she was sound asleep within minutes.

He read on for a few minutes, watching her sleep. His heart ached with feeling for this woman, this smart, beautiful and caring woman. He reached out to touch her face and drew back. He didn't want to wake her. So he sat next to the couch and watched her peaceful sleep. He was spellbound by the occasional flutter of her lashes. The tiny movements of her lips were telltale signals that thoughts were playing upon the stage of her dreams.

When her breath slowed to the faraway sound of deep sleep, he set the diary aside. There was something he had to take care of. As she slept peacefully, he slipped on his shoes, and quietly left the apartment, carefully latching the door behind him. Whoever had been here earlier, already had what they came for.

And this couldn't—no, wouldn't—wait another minute.

Chapter 33

*S*arah floated on a lake of still water, dreams swirling the events of the last week into a miasma of blood, cemeteries, dead soldiers, and torn pages of letters and diaries.

She struggled in her sleep to bring the disparate parts into order.

In a corner of her mind Rachel laughed an insane laugh, then screamed.

Jack stumbled, lost in the dark, afraid, searching.

All the images seemed related somehow.

But how?

Chapter 34

The next morning dawned with clues that had congealed in Sarah's mind during the night. Maybe the knock on the head had actually helped. She smiled to herself as she maneuvered the tight streets.

"I know where the clue is, she shouted over traffic sounds."

A few blocks away, the bells of St. Michael's chimed.

"I'm waiting," Jack said, looking at her expectantly, waiting for an answer. Part of him still half asleep.

"In the novel."

"What novel?"

"'My Heart's Still Waters.' It was with the ledgers and books the workmen put in that cardboard box. Remember?"

"Oh my God…you're right, Sarah!"

Jack and Sarah parked in the St. Philip Street parking garage and walked the two blocks to Randolph Hall. A carriage tour passed, the horses' hooves clopped on the street

148

and the tour guide's southern drawl intoned the history of the city. She had to run to keep up with Jack. *Nice man-butt,* the thought skipped through her mind.

"We have to find a way into the room," she said breathlessly as she hustled up alongside him.

He turned and grinned at her and fished around in his Dockers. "I still have a key," he said, dangling the key for her to see. "I was supposed to return it to Rachel this morning."

They had to find the novel before the diary thief did. The thief would read the diary, find the clue and come searching.

"Holt is smart. He'll make sense of all this quickly…and he says he has the sequel to the diary. We know the head at one time contained an enormous treasure."

"But Jack, we have the map. He doesn't."

The map had the phrase, Beside the Still Waters, a quasi-link to the book. They'd finished reading the diary pages she'd copied but there could have been other clues in the pages she'd not had time to copy. And they had not started yet on the letters. He picked up the pace, the key jingling in his hand as he led the way down the path and across the gravel parking lot to the old ceramics room.

"We have to find the book," she said for about the tenth time, turning it into a mantra.

"Yes. We do." He stopped and turned to her. "Or do we? Sarah, this is dangerous."

They were at the door. Should they give this chase up?

"Jack, for whatever reason, I'm supposed to be here. I'm supposed to search for the answers. I'm as sure of that as I am that it's humid here in the summer."

"Why, Sarah?"

"Honestly, I don't know. But with or without your help, I will find the answers. I have to know."

He held the keys up one more time. "Here we go."

He slipped the key into the lock and turned the handle easily. Too easily.

"It's not locked," he said.

They entered, walked the long hallway to the room. The door stood open. Inside stood Holt.

"Mr. Holt?"

"Mr. Chase."

"I believe you are trespassing, sir."

"Yes. I suppose I am. What I came for is not here. And it's not on the list of artifacts."

"How did you get in?"

"The door was open. I walked in just like you did."

"Then someone else has been here before us," Jack said to her under his breath. "You need to return the diary you stole from Ms. Singleton's apartment last evening."

"So you admit there is a diary!" Holt said, vindicated.

"You know there is and you have it," Jack said, inching closer to Holt.

"I most certainly do not have it," Holt said, his dignity impugned and his dander up. "I, sir, am a gentleman. I do not steal, unlike some people." He nodded toward her.

"Cut it out Holt. What're you looking for?"

"As I have said several times, I've come here to look for the diary. And I warned you that you could be putting yourselves in danger. Please, I beg you to give this up."

If he didn't take the diary, then who did?

"The diary was stolen earlier this evening. And whoever took it, hit Ms. Singleton—knocked her out cold. So you're saying you didn't take it?"

"My great good heavens, sir. No. And furthermore, I am not a violent man. Perhaps a little eccentric, but certainly not vicious. But I have good reason to believe that someone else with less than altruistic motives, knows about the worth of the statue's head and the importance of the diary."

"Well, don't be surprised if the police come calling. We gave them your name and a description." He believed this man had some other connection to what was going on.

Holt was aghast, huffed his outrage, then hurried out of the room. Jack made a move to follow him and Sarah grabbed his arm.

"No...Jack. He could have a gun. He's a strange little dude."

They stared at the departing Holt. She could feel Jack's body still ready to take off after Holt. "Down boy," she said tightening her hold on Jack's arm. "You okay?"

"If he didn't take the diary, who did?"

"He could've been lying,"

"I don't think so...and he said there was someone else. Someone dangerous."

Sara rubbed her arms as if she had a chill.

"We've got work to do," he said. Moving toward the worktable where the cache resided in boxes now, separated and catalogued.

"We have to find the statue head before the person who took the diary does," Jack said, and immediately started going through the items in the box.

They looked inside each book and ledger. Minutes passed as they carefully sorted through the collection, not wanting to damage the contents, hoping the novel would be among the artifacts still.

And just as quickly as they had begun, they had finished. They looked into the empty box. She couldn't believe it was bare, but it was. No book.

"Was it in the trunk?" she asked, stricken, disbelieving that an essential clue was missing. "This means someone has enough information to know how important that novel is."

"Holt must have figured out the book has a clue inside," he said.

"Jack…"

"Damn, Sarah. Maybe he took it. Hid it in his jacket when we came in."

"You may be right," Sarah said, sighing in frustration. "We need the novel."

"But…"

"What?"

"Does it have to be that copy? Maybe we can find another one somewhere."

"We're more likely to find the person who has this one than to find another copy of a book that's been out of print for more than 150 years," she said.

"The diary said the author was a professor here. And the letters."

"You're right—the letters from her lover."

She pulled the folded photocopies of the diary from her purse and flipped through several pages. Jack looked for the satchel containing the letters.

"It's gone," he said.

"What?"

"The case…" he started to panic, then saw the corner of it hiding under the tarp edge that draped from the work table into folds on the floor. He grabbed the case, looked in side, smiled up at Sarah and lifted three baggies, each containing a ribbon-tied bundle of letters.

"Whew, scared me for a minute. We have more reading to do."

Sarah looked at him skeptically. "So you're going to take the letters. You know what happened when I took the diary."

"Hey. You started this," he said grinning at her as he tucked the bags of letters inside his shirt.

"We may need these and we have no guarantee they'll be here if we come back for them."

Sarah knew he was right. She spread the photocopies of the diary out on the table.

"Here, Jack. Earlier in the diary, Charlotte talks about the book and the person who wrote it. See?" She showed him the passage. The author had been a professor at the college. "Wouldn't the college keep copies of books published by the professors who taught here?"

"Now who's the genius?" Jack asked, impressed with the notion the college could have a collection that might contain the novel. He looked at his watch. The library would be open.

He took her hand and quickly led her from the basement to the first floor and out the front door. Her tiny fingers felt small wrapped in his. Just touching her hand was comforting. Part of him wanted to find the diary, to solve the mystery of the statue and the origins of the stashed goods. But another part of him wanted to explore his growing admiration for Sarah. This sudden, unexplained need for her was unnerving. So was his instinct to flee. He wanted to be with her, but he wanted to run. He wanted to kiss her and he wanted to take the first flight out of the city. He wanted to work on the mystery and forget Sarah. He wanted to forget the mystery and turn all his attention to Sarah. He was a knotted tangle of contradictions.

"Walk or drive?" he asked.

"Walk," she said. "It'll be faster than trying to park."

They headed off across the lawn, following the wide brick skirt of the Cistern. The police tape was still up.

"This is where I found the body of that student on Monday morning," Jack said, wincing at the memory of the scene.

The Cistern was a huge circular reservoir built in the 1850s to provide water for the campus. It stood like a two-foot tall dais that served as the lawn in front of Randolph Hall. The large round saucer, banded with tabby concrete walls rose up to create a stage often used for all manner of concerts, from full orchestra offerings to small jazz combos. It was also the site each year for graduation as the young women in their white dresses carrying a single red rose and young men in their tuxedoes sporting red rose boutonnieres crossed the stage to accept their degrees.

Spanish moss hung in drapes from the massive branches of ancient oaks, helping to shield the yard from the brutal sun. Sarah walked in step with Jack as they approached the arch that led to George St.

"MS. SINGLETON!" a male voice shouted with authority.

They turned to see two policemen running toward them. One she recognized as Skeet Mallory, one of Charleston's police force.

"MS. SINGLETON!" he called to her again, making it plain he and the other officer wanted to talk to her.

"Hi Skeet. What's up?"

"Too much, Ms. S. Too much. Student killed here a few nights back. Throat cut. No leads. No sleep. And now, someone's broke into your office. Big mess, big mess. One of the students said they saw a tall man, about 6 foot-something banging on the door last night."

Skeet eyed Jack. So did Sarah. She had awakened this morning to Jack coming in the door, a grocery bag in tow. He said he'd gone to get some coffee and some Krispy Kremes. Which he had. They'd eaten them before leaving the apartment.

"Mr. Chase, we meet again. Thank you for speaking to the Duncans yesterday at headquarters. Meant a lot them."

"The Duncans?" Sarah looked at Jack, the questions mounting.

"Mr. Chase discovered Craig Duncan's body," he pointed to the cistern lawn, "Over there."

Sarah went pale. "Craig. The student who was killed was Craig Duncan?"

"Yes ma'am. Very sad. You knew him?"

She nodded yes. "He was doing research for the building renovation for Mr. Atkinson, the project manager and my boss Rachel Stover."

Sarah looked from Jack to Skeet, and knew it was time to be afraid.

"I'll need you two to come down to headquarters," Mallory said.

"Can we do this later today?"

"No ma'am. Afraid not. Rachel Stover is at headquarters insisting you stole some kind of diary that belongs to the college, Ms. Singleton. She said Mr. Chase might be in on it."

Sarah and Jack locked eyes. How did Rachel even know about the diary?

"Skeet. Mr. Chase has been with me the last 24 hours. You've got the wrong man."

"Were you with him at dark-thirty this morning as well? Ms. Stover seems to think you were the one who took the diary from the school, ma'am. Says you were mad at her and helped Mr. Chase here steal college property to get back at her."

Sarah could see that continuing the conversation was futile.

They would have to go down to headquarters and get this cleared up. And Craig Duncan? He was a good kid. Smart. Had he discovered something? Her skin rippled.

An hour later as they sat at Skeet Mallory's desk describing Holt to the detective for the third time, Sarah's patience gave way to remembrance.

"Skeet. I couldn't have been tearing up my office last night. I was at my apartment being assaulted. There'll be a report of it. EMS was called. And a couple of your officers were there. And Jack was with me the whole time."

"What time was that?"

"The police and EMS were there for at least a few hours. From about 9 p.m. until midnight or later. Jack took me to the hospital to get checked out, then we came home."

Mallory took notes, squinted up at her. "What about after that. What time did Chase leave?

"He stayed with me at my apartment,"

Mallory looked up at her, a snarky knowing look on his face.

"It's not like that. He cleaned up the mess left by the person who tore my place apart. It could be the same person who tore up the office."

"We'll check it out. Any alibi other than each other that you were in your apartment all night." Skeet eyed here suspiciously.

"About 2 a.m. my landlady came up to check on me. I had a concussion from being hit on the head, and she wanted to be sure I was okay. And she can vouch for Jack, too. He was still shelving my books. He was there all night."

"Well, then we have a real problem, cause Ms. Stover says Mr. Chase was with her starting at about 4:30 a.m. 'til after sunrise."

"That's preposterous," Sarah practically shouted. She looked at Jack, certain he would be as outraged at the suggestion as she was. But he wasn't. He looked at her like he wanted to disappear.

"Sarah, I can explain."

A voice from behind them chimed in.

"Yes, Jack. Explain to her about how, as soon as you knew she was asleep, you came knocking on my door. Tell her all about it."

Sarah turned to see Rachel standing in the doorway, hands on her hips, jaw set and a smile playing across her face. What was Rachel talking about—why wasn't he denying her accusation. Surely, she had misread the guilt on his face.

"Jack?" she asked weakly. She honestly couldn't believe what she was hearing. Her conscious mind could see it was true, but her heart was screaming "NO!" She finally got her lips to work.

"Did you go to her house last night, Jack?"

Sarah's heart pounded with the exertion of trying to breathe. *Seriously?* She'd begun to respect this man, to think of him as a partner in her quest for the truth about the statue. But her first instinct was right. He was a player just like Rachel told her. And now he'd proved it. *He waited until I was asleep and went to Rachel's house?*

"Would you two mind waiting in here?" Detective Mallory asked. "And Ms. Stover, if you would please have a seat over there."

He ushered Jack and Sarah into an adjacent room and closed the door. I'll need to see that backpack Mr. Chase. Just a quick look to be sure there are no weapons or contraband. Mallory took the bag and left them.

They sat in total silence for a few seconds.

"Sarah…"

She refused to look at him and fought the urge to scream. She was exhausted and a little scared. Tears were a real possibility if she spoke at all. With whom had she aligned herself?

After a few minutes, Jack pulled one of the stacks of letters from his shirt and slipped the ribbon knot loose. He opened the envelope of the first one and carefully pulled the folded pages out.

"We still have a mystery to solve."

She wanted to hit him.

Sarah glanced at the letter he unfolded on the table. The script was beautiful, but masculine. It had a stronger flourish than Charlotte's. He read it aloud to her.

My Sweet Charlotte,

How I long for the day we can be together again. I miss you more with each passing moment, as the war rages on around me, I long for the times we stood by the Cistern reading poetry or my silly first attempts at writing. I remember with such nostalgia the days when I was your professor and you, my student, sitting eagerly in the classroom. My novel was my heart's desire for us. Please know the words I wrote within about the hero and heroine are a thinly veiled analogy for us.

Often in my mind is the night we spent together before my departure. The memory of your warm embrace and your welcoming love are with me constantly. I feel you with me as I struggle through the long nights without you.

We are going into another battle today. We have cleaned our rifles and have prepared for the worst. I know I chose to fight in this war, and I know that it was the right thing to do. But I also know now what I did not understand before. I truly may not return from this battle. And for the first time, I have such sadness at the thought of you enduring the news of my demise. I hope these feelings do not portend what is to come, but merely a manifest of the fear all around me. If this letter finds you, it will convey my affection for you and my dream that we be reunited someday soon to live out our days together as husband and wife.

With deepest love and affection,
Your own true love,
Jeremiah

How could Jack sit there calmly reading aloud this love letter?

"Sweet." Jack said. "Jeremiah was deeply in love and probably scared half to death. He was a professor. A writer, for crying out loud."

"Jack please..." She didn't want to hear anything about Jeremiah. She didn't want to hear Jack's voice reading the letters.

"He didn't know anything about people shooting at each other," Jack continued.

She didn't respond. There was nothing to say to him. Footsteps approached the room and Jack bound her eyes to his. Precognition—that's what she saw in his face.

"I'm so sorry, Sarah. It really isn't what you think. I know how lame that sounds. But truth is, it just isn't."

Skeet returned, earnest, efficient, strictly business. Gone was the amiable city cop. He returned the small backpack to Jack.

He asked Sarah a few more innocuous questions about her interactions with Holt.

"Sarah, you can go now. Mr. Chase will have to stick

around a while longer. We have a few more questions."

As angry as Sarah was, and frightened, she was hesitant to leave him there. Something didn't feel right. In fact everything felt wrong. She wasn't sure what the truth was, but she was pretty darned sure it wasn't what it appeared on the surface.

Reluctantly she stood to leave.

"Sarah?" Jack's face betrayed his distress. With his back to Mallory, and facing her, he slipped the letters into his backpack and handed it to her.

With a final glance, she left him sitting there in the faded green room with Detective Mallory. As she rounded the corner to the lobby, it was Rachel's worried face she saw disappear behind closing elevator doors.

Sarah stood there for a few seconds.

"What was really happening here?"

Chapter 35

The library sign read, "closed."

Sarah sighed in frustration and headed home. It would have to wait until tomorrow. The entire afternoon had been wasted at the station as Detective Mallory grilled her and Jack.

And then there was Rachel. Sarah had more questions than answers.

She curled up on the sofa and pulled the pale lavender satin ribbon loose from the second bundle of letters and slipped the page from the brittle envelope. A rose petal fell into her lap followed by several more as she opened the pages. Delicate, dried petals. Had they once been pink? She carefully returned them to the envelope.

Dear Sweet Charlotte,

Enclosed are petals from a rose I found on the side of the road as we marched toward battle yesterday. I saw the beauty of it and was reminded of your sweetness. I know that by the time you receive them, the petals will be dry, but they will still contain the love that has sent them your way. My dear sweet Charlotte, when your letter arrived yesterday, my soul was gladdened by the words within. News of your family's departure from the city was alarming, but I am happy you will be in a safer location. And you will be nearer to me. If luck holds, maybe I will be able to make my way to you for a few days respite. I know this is the silly dream of a soldier who is homesick. The hills of North Carolina are relatively quiet so far, but the winters are more brutal than you are familiar with. I hope you have taken your warmest clothing. Your father's forethought for the family's future was as intelligent as always. He was also wise not to carry much on the journey. I can't imagine your sadness at leaving your beautiful home but am quite worried that you had to separate from your father during the escape. How terrifying to be stopped. I wonder at your courage in escaping the carriage and safely burying your "future." I know the place to which you allude, the place that has already known sadness for our family and destruction from the great fire. This is a place that cannot be carried away or moved by any force of war.

I cannot bear the thought you would not survive the war, but I know where the wall is that your father had built. He showed me the plans before I was deployed. I will look for the map inside the diary you have hidden in the secret room should I return to Charleston before you do. I will hold it safe as a record of our lives there before the war. I look forward to the day when we can read your memory book together and reestablish our lives with the remaining treasure that 'lies within' as we begin our lives together as man and wife."

The plan to hide your goods is an excellent one. From the tales

I've heard, many who have tried to carry all their belongings have either had to abandon their treasures along the way, or have been killed in their defense. Travel light with Godspeed to your new location, my love. I will find you after this horrible war has ended, and sooner if I can find a way to do so, and our lives can resume.

With much love and affection
Your humble, homesick soldier,
Jeremiah

The Beaufain family moved to North Carolina. To the mountains—possibly near her own home!

A sharp knock on the door shattered her silence. She dropped the letter. She gathered the pages and moved The Post and Courier to hide the bundles.

"Who is it?"

"It's me," came the voice from beyond the door.

She quickly opened the door and stepped aside for him to enter.

"I wasn't sure you'd even speak to me," he said coming quickly into the room.

"Something isn't making sense," she said, wanting very much to tell him what she'd just discovered in the letter, but needing to know why he'd gone to Rachel's even more.

"I went to Rachel's house to talk to her. She doesn't sleep, you know. She never has," he said.

"Rachel's sleep habits are of no interest…"

"It's part of her manic personality. There was a time when I found that fascinating. Now I find it sad and strange."

"Whatever Jack. Get to the point."

"She can hurt you. I asked her to let us finish the project. I asked her to act like a normal human being."

"That's asking a lot, Jack."

"Rachel seemed afraid. Her mouth was saying one thing but her demeanor was off."

Sarah understood exactly what he was saying. Something wasn't ringing true with Rachel.

"I asked her if she had taken the diary. And she laughed, nervous. Wouldn't look me in the eye. Wouldn't answer."

He turned to face Sarah and leaned down to look at her eye-to-eye.

"I left. I wasn't getting anywhere. And I didn't wreck the office."

"I never thought you wrecked the office, Jack. That's not your style," she said. He turned back to the window and she stood watching his back, and the harbor beyond.

"Sarah, I have to say something."

When he spoke again it was slowly and so softly she had to move closer to hear him.

"You matter to me, Sarah. I knew that for sure this afternoon when you walked out of the station," he said, still looking out the window.

"I've been worried something would happen to you before I could get back here," and when he turned to look at her, she knew he meant it.

"I tried to explain as much as I could to Mallory, but I don't think I got through to him about what's going on. It doesn't make a whole lot of sense, even to me." He shook his head in frustration.

Something in his voice chilled her. He was deadly serious.

"I'm listening," she said, her words almost as hushed as his.

"I have an idea about the statue head."

Did she want to continue with this project? The link to Craig Duncan's murder had her spooked.

She needed to think. She turned and went up the staircase

to the widow's walk. The humid night air enveloped her like arms comforting a scared child. Was she strong enough to turn her back on the diary's message? The statue? Or was she strong enough to continue with the project? Either way it took more strength than she was convinced she had.

She wanted to stand here and be swept by the air, by the boats leaving the harbor for exotic ports. A container ship sounded its horn as it moved across the harbor. She could go downstairs right now, grab her purse, a couple of credit cards and fly anywhere in the world and start a new life. She had no one to answer to. The consequences of so dramatic a change would affect only her. There was no one and nothing to worry about, only her houseplants—and Mrs. B would love to have them to care for. Her life was virtually devoid of encumbrances. It was the way she wanted it. The specter of a more involved life, a life filled with relationships, had haunted her from time to time, like now. But she'd always been strong enough to say no and move on. But now she was questioning that strength. And as for her father's request, she would send him the money from her savings. If she left here she would go far away and not let him or her brothers know where she'd gone.

But how much backbone did it really take to live a solitary life?

Jack was a lot of trouble. That was obvious. He'd unsettled her from the moment they met at the arts center. And now she felt real fear in the wake of learning Craig Duncan was the murder victim. It had to be related to the treasure. It would be too big of a coincidence for it to be otherwise.

His footsteps on the spiral staircase forced a decision.

And then his presence next to her at the railing resigned

her to speak. The lights atop the Ravenel Bridge glowed over the confluence of the Cooper and Wando rivers. And as a container ship slipped through the jetties into the Atlantic the desire to leave tugged at her heart. She wanted to run. To go far away.

"You really went to her house after I fell asleep?"

"Yes."

"Jack, what were you thinking?" She looked at him for half a second and returned her gaze to the dark harbor.

Silence hung between them, dividing them. The project was important to her professionally.

"I will work with you on the project. Please don't ask more of me."

"I care about you."

"I will not be involved with someone who's interested in what amounts to nothing more than self-gratification."

The resigned look on his face said he would do as she asked.

"My only interest is in finding the head of the statue." She looked at him defiantly.

"Yes. I understand."

How dare he look so crestfallen.

"The library is closed for the night. We'll meet in the morning and start over."

"What time?"

"The library opens at seven o'clock. Meet me there."

"Sarah? "

"Seven o'clock, Jack, at the library. Let's get this over with as soon as possible."

She watched as he left, breathed a sigh of relief and of disappointment, and listened as his footsteps faded into the night on the sidewalk below.

Chapter 36

Jack threw the room key on the table and pulled off his shirt. The day had been long, irritating and had ended miserably. But as bad as it was, it could have been worse. At least Sarah agreed to see him in the morning and they could still work together. At least for tomorrow. He didn't blame her. How could he? He'd kept the truth from her, not trusting her to believe him, not even considering the impact of keeping things from her. And how ridiculous to have gone to Rachel's house in the middle of the night. She was right. What had he been thinking?

The shower flowed over his body washing away the tension of a day that had gone on way too long. Sarah seemed within him and all around him. The water rushed down his chest, between his legs, caressed him, stroked his body. He let the water work its magic on him as he gave in to the warmth, to the need. Finally spent he sighed heavily, soaped down one more time and rinsed away the rest of the day. By the time he wrapped the towel around his waist and brushed his teeth, he felt more in charge of himself.

He would lie down on top of the covers for a few minutes, then he'd get up and make a few notes on the day. But as he lay there the thoughts of Sarah crowded his mind: her smiling face, her deeply Southern accent, her glorious tangle of hair and sea green eyes. And intelligence. He finally let sleep overtake him. A swirl of ocean and sex and brittle letters and soldiers and Sarah formed a whirlwind in his restless mind.

When his cell phone jarred him awake, he'd lost all sense of time and place. He scanned the room, reorienting himself and spying the clock. 5 a.m.

"Who the hell," he muttered, then added, "Who do you think dumb ass," answering himself. He started not to pick up, but then thought, what if it was Sarah?

"Hello?"

"Jackie, dearest."

"Rachel," he said flatly. "What do you want?"

"I have something you want."

"I doubt that very much."

Her voice changed. It sounded as if she were reading something.

"Father and mother have packed our trunks with only the most useful of our goods. My green ashes dress was folded in paper and placed near the top. Mother has been weeping, although she tries to hide it from me."

"You bitch. You have the diary. You actually broke into Sarah's apartment and stole the diary. And you hurt her. I wouldn't have thought even you would sink that low."

"A little like the pot calling the kettle black isn't it. After all, she stole it from the college."

168

"Damn it Rachel."

"I was simply recovering something for which I was responsible and that had been pilfered by your hillbilly."

"You hurt her, Rachel. She had to go to the hospital."

Rachel didn't say anything for couple of beats, then, with a voice tight as a tick said, "Wasn't me, Jack."

"You just said you took the ..."

"I did. But I didn't see Sarah at all. I was on the street when you drove up. I saw you."

More silence.

"Someone else was there. I left when I did because I heard someone outside." He voice was quiet. The goading, superior edge gone.

"It seems I'm not the only person who is less than enamored of your girlfriend."

"She's not my girlfriend. So what do you want now, Rachel?"

"I want you to come and get the diary. I don't want it. You should take it...take it to the police."

"Why?"

"I'm bored with the whole thing." Jack knew there was more to it. More she wasn't saying.

"This situation is tiresome. In fact, you are tiresome, Jack. You used to be fun, and now you're every old man who ever hit on me. Pathetic and boring. If you want the hick, you can have her. You belong together."

"You really are a bitch," Jack said, spitting out the words like he would a bad oyster.

"So do you want it—the diary—or shall I give it to Holt when he gets here?"

"You wouldn't."

"Why wouldn't I?"

"Don't give it to Holt. I'll be there in a few minutes to pick it up."

"See you then sweet thing."

Jack grabbed the key and headed once more to Rachel's house. He called Sarah to tell her what was happening but the line went straight to voicemail. He knew this was the right thing to do this time—even Sarah would agree it was. They needed the diary.

Rachel's house was only a couple of blocks from the hotel so he decided to walk. The breeze he felt atop the widow's walk earlier was missing on dark narrow Bedon's Alley, the small downtown enclave of antebellum houses and cobblestone streets. The city sounds were subdued. No music drifted on this early morning air. No frogs croaked their contentment. But the humid air enveloped him, seeped through his clothes, clinging to his skin. The only sound was that of his own heartbeat. Charleston was all around him and working its way into his psyche. He loved this place. And on this street, in the grayness before sunrise, he knew he was growing to love Sarah.

Gas streetlamps flickered, casting uneven shadows on the walls and bushes that lined the walled street. Light spilled onto the narrow lane up ahead, the source at first unknown to him. As he approached, he could see it was coming from Rachel's window. His footsteps sounded monstrously loud on the damp cobbles echoing in the silence of predawn.

Rachel's door was open, he assumed in expectation of his arrival. *Damn. He'd have to go inside.* She was probably in the den all the way in the back of the house.

The narrow hallway led him past expensive paintings and through a 20-foot length of greenhouse wall before emerging into the kitchen and the den just beyond. The side yard was barely visible through the condensation on the expanse of floor-to-ceiling windows that formed one wall of the den. The effect was of a garden in the living space. The garden door was open. The damp, warm air mixed with the air-conditioned draft that blew against his back from the overhead vent.

"Rachel?" silence greeted him. He picked up a pencil from the counter, tapping it on the marble bar. His nerves began to twang.

He called to her, "I came for the diary. Don't fool around." Again, silence. Tree frogs had found their voice and croaked lazily in the garden. "You can either come out or I'm leaving. Now." He dropped the pencil. The sound clattered through the empty room.

He turned to leave, not willing to play her games. How stupid could one man be to fall for this shit again? *Always hopeful. No. Always gullible.*

"I'm leaving now, Rachel." His steps rang hollow on the slate floor. The hot humid night rolled into the den with the heavy scent of wet earth and lush foliage from the open garden door as the air conditioner clicked off. He surveyed the kitchen, giving her more time to come out from wherever she was hiding, probably watching him and laughing to herself. He opened the refrigerator, a habit that was hard to break. Not a lot inside. A few pieces of fruit and a bottle of wine. It looked like what he'd expect of her. He pushed it shut and walked over to close the garden door, when a noise in the garden stopped him. He listened, his hand on the knob. Nothing. He began to push the door shut.

"Jac.." he heard a faint voice. It came from the garden. He pushed the door open again and walked onto the damp grass.

"Is someone here?" A chorus of tree frogs croaked. "Rachel?"

Jack's skin crawled. Something felt wrong. Very wrong. "Rachel?"

The hair on the back of his neck stood up.

Light from the den streamed in ribbons through the bushes to illuminate bits of the small yard. And then he saw it—a bare foot. His insides froze into a knot. All the air sucked out of his lungs.

"Rachel," he said in a hoarse whisper and went over to her crumpled body and brushed the hair from her face. Her eyes fluttered open, a stream of blood oozed from her neck.

"Ja..." She coughed and gripped his hand. "Diary...took it. The man. She gripped his arm and struggled for a breath. Go...go..."

"Don't move," he said, and noticed the dark of night had eased in the few minutes since he'd come into the house. He looked at his watch. 5:40 a.m. Everything had the gray, flat look of predawn. Details were indistinct.

A noise. Someone was in the den. Holt?

"Miss Barbara?" a sing-song voice called in the den. It was the housekeeper, Minnie. Jack had met her before. She came early every morning to prepare breakfast and get a start on the day.

He knew she'd seen him when he heard a little cry pierce the frog-croaking. "WHO ARE YOU?" she shouted, her light Gullah accent taking on a panicked tone. Jack looked once more at Rachel. Then back at the housekeeper who suddenly had the look of recognition on her face. *She knows me.*

Rachel pulled on his arm.

"Craig...so sorry," she whispered.

"Rachel..." She was breathing easily. Why was she talking about Craig?

"Map." Rachel's eyes closed, exhausted from the effort of

breathing.

"Go, Jack. Go. Sarah's in danger."

He looked up at the housekeeper's face, distorted by fear and by the condensation on the windows through which he could see her. She was punching numbers into her cell phone. He pulled himself up and bolted through the door. Minnie's screams faded as he ran down the cobbled street, stumbled and regained his footing. He leaned in the dark against an antique brick wall and he too punched in 911. Breathlessly he reported the assault and Rachel's address, but clicked off as the operator asked his identity. He let out a tiny yelp when a cat jumped from the wall behind him and loped across the street, sliding under a wrought iron driveway gate.

"Damn," he swore under his breath, his nerves frayed and unraveling. He should have stayed with Rachel. But she said to go. That Sarah was in danger. And Minnie was there. A siren grew closer and he peered through a bush to see it come to a stop in front of Rachel's Bedon's Alley home. Okay. It'll be okay. They'll take care of her.

And then he was running. Running down Meeting Street, closing the ground between him and The Mills House and a shower and a change of clothes and Sarah. He would be with Sarah at the library when it opened. He needed time. Just a little time. They'd be after him soon. His name would emerge pretty quickly, but maybe not so soon he and Sarah couldn't solve what needed to be solved and find what needed to be found. Between now and the police finding him, which they surely would, he had work to do. He called Sarah, told her to go down and stay with Mrs. B.

"Jack? What's going on?"

"Just do it Sarah...and meet me at the library at seven. And please be careful."

In the meantime he needed to know what Craig Duncan had found. What he'd been killed for.

There was only one person he could think of who might be able to help.

Chapter 37

Jack Chase turned the lamp on in the not-quite-daybreak-still-dark workroom, rubbed his eyes and sipped the strong Biggby coffee he'd picked up on the way in. All the parts to this puzzle floated in the air like confetti at a ticker-tape parade. At some point it would all start to make sense but right now he couldn't see the pattern, the rhythm that would give him direction to solve this one.

A door clicked at the far end of the hall. Had the building not been so quietly empty, he wouldn't have heard it at all. The footsteps were equally subtle, almost hesitant. He couldn't see anyone yet, too far away, just out of view, but creeping closer. He leaned against the worktable, hands anchored on either side waiting for her arrival, heart pounding just a little harder than normal. He had a steak knife from the restaurant he'd pilfered as he left. It wasn't much, but it was better than bare fists.

The honeyed hair told him who the visitor was: the very sad Emily Randall. He pulled a file folder over the knife, just out of her sight.

She stood in his door, uncertainty and determination scrawled on her face. Grief for Craig Duncan, her lost love, was etched into her young face.

"Miss Randall. Come in." He moved towards her and motioned to the first of two metal chairs near the window. He took the one next to it as she sat down and started talking, words spilling out into the dimly lit room.

"Craig. Craig told me something. And it might not mean anything. It might not matter. It seems silly now, but maybe not, but he told me something. He told me…and I dreamed it in my sleep. I was going to tell the police in the morning…and you called and…"

Jack leaned forward. "Take a deep breath and tell me," he said calmly. The thumping inside his chest seemed audible.

"He said he had something he wanted to show me. Something I would get a kick out of."

"Did he say what it was?"

"He said it was one of my favorite things and that he discovered it and had sold it to a man, but wanted me to see it first."

"Where. Did he say where he discovered it?"

"I can't remember. I think he said something about the research he was doing for the renovation. And he said something about a woman named Rachel. Something about a secret room. At first I thought maybe it was a coin or an artifact from the Civil War. He was teasing me about it. But Civil War social history is my area of study and he knows I love that stuff. He sounded excited about it."

She dabbed at her eyes and took a ragged breath.

"The day I was at the police station, I went through the contents of Craig's backpack with Det. Mallory."

"Was there anything, a clue to what he might have wanted to show you?"

"Craig said what he found was romantic...oh. Oh my. He said it was romantic. I'd forgotten. A letter. I think he said something about a letter."

She shook her head as if trying not to think about anything romantic. She looked him in the eye then looked away, tears pooling in her enormous eyes.

"But the only thing in the backpack that was at all interesting was a scrap of paper, quite old. It had a few markings on it."

Jack's skin prickled tight.

Chapter 38

Jack was nearly hidden behind a tree, sitting on the wall that bordered the landscaping of the library when she drove up, parked across the street and skirted traffic to join him.

"Let's hope they have what we came for," she said crisply. She felt, rather than saw, him fall in step with her.

"Sarah, something happened last night…this morning. I tried to call. Your phone was off."

"What? What happened? Another late night meeting with Rachel?"

His silence said more than words ever could have. He stopped walking. When she realized he was no longer with her, she turned.

"Really? Are you absolutely insane?"

"She called. Said she had the diary and if I didn't come and get it she would give it to Holt."

"So you actually went to Rachel's again?"

"When I got there the door was open. She was in the

garden, badly injured."

Sarah walked back to where he was standing, her eyes wide, not leaving his. His face was ashen.

"She said a man had taken the diary. He hit her, kicked her, had started to cut her throat but ran when he heard me call to her from the front door."

"Oh my God...Holt?" Sarah instinctively grabbed Jack's forearm.

"I don't think so. She would have said, 'Holt,' and not 'the man.'"

"How badly hurt is she?"

"The housekeeper came in. I ran, called 911 from across the street and stayed to be sure they arrived to care for her."

"So you left her?"

"She said something. 'Craig. Map. So sorry.'"

Sarah looked out across the street, surveyed their surroundings, then looked up at the entrance.

"She told me to go. That you were in danger. She said it twice."

He looked at her, worry creasing his brow, his usually light brown eyes, now dark.

"I met with Emily Randall last night."

"Emi...Craig's girlfriend?" Sarah swallowed hard. This was becoming increasingly dangerous. "You had a busy night."

"Yeah. When she and Mallory went through the contents of Craig's backpack, she said there was a scrap of paper."

Jack reached into his pocket and pulled out his phone. He held it up for her to see the photo of a scrap of paper.

"Mallory allowed her to make a copy of it...thought she might be able to help him figure out what it was. She wouldn't give me the copy but let me take a photo of it."

"Jack! It's the rest of the map." She pulled out the piece of map from the baggy.

"We need answers, and I need your help to get them."

He looked up at the library.

"We need to find the book, put all of this together, and figure out where Charlotte buried the head.

"Craig was killed over something he found," Sarah said.

"Emily thinks it was a letter, but I think we may have the most important thing that Craig had right here." Jack held up the phone.

"And whoever attacked Sarah wants the answers too and won't mind killing us for it."

Chapter 39

The Addleston library was a beautiful new building that housed historic collections as well a modern computer system and vast library for students and visitors. It had been open for only a few years. *Please, let them have the book.*

Sarah led the way up the steps into the cool interior of the library. Her friend Michelle stood behind the desk.

"Yes," she whispered to Jack with relief. "Come on, Jack. Luck just might be with us."

"Hi, Michelle," Sarah said as calmly as possible, not missing Michelle's appraisal of Jack. Michelle rolled her eyes from Jack to Sarah, lifted an eyebrow and whispered, "You go, girl."

"Michelle, this is Jack Chase. He's an art authenticator and we need your help. It's really important."

"Sure, Sarah. If I can."

"Is there a collection of books written by professors of the college?"

"Sure there is. We have them in a room upstairs. Getting published is real important to those guys you know."

"Would you have the really old ones—like from the 1800s?"

"Are you kidding, Sarah. This city thrives on old; the older the better. Karen—I'm going upstairs for a few minutes," Michelle said to her co-worker.

Minutes later they were pouring over the shelves of books in a glass-walled room on the third floor.

"I'll leave you two to find what you need. These books have to stay here. But if you need a copy of something, well, there you go," she said, pointing to the fancy new Xerox as she slipped through the door and disappeared down the hall.

"There're so many," Jack said, surveying the room.

"Yes. Lots of books," she said flatly. "You take that side and I'll take this side." For several minutes they scanned the shelves. Most were recent works: Brett Lott's novels, Scott Poole's *Monsters in America,* Jack Bass' look at Strom Thurmond, Peeple's works on Edgar Allan Poe who was tied to the Lowcountry through the time he spent on Sullivan's Island writing *The Gold Bug.* On a corner shelf near the back of the small room were the very old books.

And then suddenly it was there, an exact duplicate of the novel that had been stolen. Her heart raced as she lifted the dark leather-bound volume, "It's here," Sarah said, holding it in both hands and doing a little dance.

"I don't believe it," Jack said. "This was almost too easy." On the cover was the title, "My Heart's Still Waters."

She flipped through the first few pages and got quiet. "We don't really know what we're looking for."

"The book has to have a location that matches the place she buried the head," Jack said. "And I'll bet it's some place with still waters."

Sarah nodded in agreement as she continued fingering through the brittle pages, scanning each, looking for any reference to water.

In a passage describing the heroine and the hero meeting for a midnight tryst, Sarah stopped, and read.

"His dark eyes caressed her white skin as they fell into each others arms, alone together at last, escapees from the twirling of the dancers and the frenetic sound of the orchestra. They had met here before by chance, but tonight, the meeting was planned. Annabelle felt supported by the dark still waters beneath their feet. It was her favorite place. She had run around it as a child and now stood here on it as an adult. It was the place she'd come to think and to study.

"What's she talking about?" Jack said. "If she's standing on it, it can't be an open body of water unless she's standing on a pier or dock."

"It doesn't sound like that," she said. "It's something that contains water. So it must have some kind of top on it."

She turned the next page and read forward.

"Jack, I know where the head is."

"Where?"

The Cistern."

"The Cistern?" he said, recognition dawning. "Sarah you're a genius. You're right! It has to be The Cistern."

Sarah pulled the scrap of map from her pocket. She'd slipped it into a baggie before they left the apartment and now handled it carefully, examining it through the clear plastic. Now that they had an idea where the starting point was, the map made a lot more sense.

"This must be the Porter's Lodge arch leading onto the lawn where The Cistern is," she said, pointing to a semicircular drawing. "And here...this is The Cistern. It has to be. And we were just there. We might have walked right over the top of it!"

A door slammed at the end of the hall. Sarah jumped. So did Jack. Nerves were skittish.

"I think you're right," Jack said, gently taking the baggie from her and looking at the map himself. "Let's go, Sarah. We need to hurry."

Something in his tone, his manner, had changed. Tense, jumpy. Every noise made him start. She went to return the book to the shelf, but slipped it into her purse instead. She was turning into a regular book thief. She would apologize to Michelle later. This was more important than library rules.

They hurried out the side entrance. They had to get to The Cistern before Rachel or Holt.

Chapter 40

The Cistern was relatively quiet today. A few students straggled along the outside sidewalk. A woman sat on a bench near the entrance arch reading The Post and Courier with her red longhair dachshund lounging in the cool grass at her feet. There was no one else in the enclosed area.

Sarah and Jack covered the short distance to the raised lawn that was The Cistern. The antique brick walkway was slightly uneven. They took the three steps up to the brick path that split The Cistern lawn in half.

"Now what?" Jack asked scanning the surroundings for any signs that someone was after him. He expected any minute to be surrounded by a hoard of police with drawn guns.

He'd spent more than one afternoon lounging on the grass here, with one coed or another, pretending to learn French or calculus while fingering a well-lotioned leg and planting light kisses on décolletage. He looked back to Sarah. Beautiful Sarah. His past seemed like a cheesy movie about some other person. He was so far removed from the man he started out to be. That was never more apparent than it was this very moment. And Sarah was so different than any woman he started out to find. It felt good to be this man. He wanted to rewind his decision to go to Rachel's early this morning. But at the same time, the visit may have set them on the track to finding out who had killed Craig Duncan, and where the statue's head was. And it likely saved her life.

"Sarah."

She looked up from the map, her brow creased with the effort of trying to locate the markers on the paper and reconciling it with the image on Jack's phone.

"Hmmm?"

He cleared his throat and took the map from her. "I guess we better figure this out."

"This doesn't really fit, Jack. I was so sure this was the right place. It only made sense the still waters were The Cistern. But now I'm not so sure. What are all these markings?"

Several irregular rows of notches dotted the map, the circular edge they'd believed to be The Cistern now looked to be only part of the answer or not the answer at all.

"I think this is the starting place that will lead us to another location. See, this looks like the curve here. But what's this on the other side?" Jack said.

"We need to read the rest of the letters. I still think this is a map of where the head is buried. We just need to rethink the location."

"And the book," she said, pulling from her purse the small, soft leather-bound book.

They were exposed here in the open.

"This doesn't feel real smart to me, sitting out here in plain view. And if anyone is looking for us, your apartment isn't the best choice either."

"My apartment is not an option under any circumstance," she said coldly.

"Of course not."

"Do you know G&M, Fast and French? It's out of the way and the back corners are relatively private," Sarah suggested.

"Perfect." He knew the small hole-in-the-wall French restaurant. It'd been a fixture on Broad Street for many years, as popular with students and locals as it was with tourists. It had a definite European quality in addition to nooks and crannies in which one could have a private conversation. Soups, breads, cheeses, wine and strong coffees were their specialties, but a full menu of French dishes were proclaimed daily on the chalkboard.

He hoped they would be safe and private there. Jack had spent more than one afternoon sipping wine and getting hot with a particular dark haired woman—a professor—in the back alcove. Every corner of Charleston was a memory of one woman or another. Yet the only one he needed, the one he was with right now, wanted nothing to do with him.

And now he was counting the minutes until the police found him.

Chapter 41

$\mathcal{J}$ ack and Sarah retrieved her convertible and parked near the tiny restaurant on Broad Street. Inside was relatively quiet but alive with the aromas of French press coffee, cheese, bread and savory soups.

They squeezed past the counter and the tourist couple sitting there. A trio of students giggled a few seats down. An elderly couple sipped coffee at the counter near the front. He was relieved his favorite spot in the back was empty. They slipped into the bench seat, she as close to the wall as she could get, making it plain she wanted to be as far away from him as possible.

He spread out several of the letters on the sturdy tabletop.

They poured over them, looking for any mention of the statue. The author of the letters had been in a battle, he longed for Charlotte and the comforts of home.

"Your sweet smile brightens my dreams, Sweet Charlotte. Today, my friend Folen was killed in battle. One minute we were

side by side, charging forward, the next he was lying on the ground,
his eyes staring up at the heaven that I am sure he is in right now.
The horrors of this war cannot be truly told, because it is so ghastly.
My heart yearns for you and is with you always, even though I am
not. Dear Charlotte, fear not for me, for the Lord is with me. He
leadeth me beside the still waters where my beloved father rests.
With great love and affection,
Jeremiah

"Still waters again. That could be important, Sarah."

Sarah took out a notebook and jotted down the date of the
letter and examined the front of the envelope. She turned it
over. On the back was the name of the sender, Jeremiah
Singleton.

"Jack, look." She showed him the envelope.

"A relative?"

"Not likely…we're mountain folk, you know. From back
in the hills. Not very sophisticated." She fixed him with a
stony stare.

Jack flinched. He'd disappointed her more than he
realized. *You reap what you sow and I've sown a lot of ill will*
with a whole lot of women.

"Let's look at everything together," he said, pulling the
other letters from his backpack, and she deposited the book on
the table along with the photocopies of the diary.

The waiter took their order for coffee, a plate of cheeses,
fruit and a baguette. They were hungry, anxious and intrigued.

He read a couple more letters, identifying strongly with
Jeremiah's wish to be with the woman he loved. He was sitting
next to the woman his gut told him was the one for him, yet
felt as far away from Sarah as Jeremiah felt from Charlotte.
And he, too, was waiting for the next volley of shots to be fired.

The Diary

"Listen to this," Sarah said and began to read from the last few photocopied pages of Charlotte's diary.

"I have waited to write these words when I had a quiet place to do so. My family has gone ahead after being detained. I did not write of this some weeks ago for fear my family might read of this should I be killed, but now, with the shelling all around me, and my future so uncertain, I want this remembrance of the love Jeremiah and I shared to find a home among my other thoughts. I am alone in the world, but will leave Charleston tomorrow to join my family in North Carolina. I am staying at The Mills House. My uncle, Joseph Purcell, is the proprietor and promised my father I could stay safely at his establishment until I depart.

Jeremiah and I spent our last moments together here. On the night before his regiment left, I became Jeremiah's completely. We could not bear to part unjoined. Father forbade us to marry. He does not want me to be a young widow of this war. But in our hearts Jeremiah and I already are married, and now in our bodies we also are joined. We met last night at the ruins of the Circular Church. It was very late, but we slipped into the shell of the church and went to where the altar once had been and knelt there. My dear Jeremiah and I exchanged vows before God and in our hearts. He slipped his grandmother's gold wedding band onto my finger. We are now one, both in spirit and in the flesh.

He had taken a room at The Mills House. Uncle Joseph gave him the room since there are so few guests in what feels like the end of Charleston.

As Jeremiah held me in the early morning hours, I held back my tears. I wanted to be as brave as he for going forward into the most horrible war. I know he thinks it is right, but I am but a woman, and I wish he were not going. But still, he is noble and a patriot. I am proud but yet a little angry that I am not enough to hold him here. And my knowledge that he will not return seems certain, not a superstition as he says.

He insisted I wait in the room as he left, but once he'd gone, I slipped from The Mills House and followed. I nearly fainted when I saw Uncle Joseph turn the corner down the hall. The scandal of being discovered in a hotel at this hour would be devastating to my family even in these distressing times. But I could not give up even one second that we could be together, or that I could rest my eyes on his dear face. When he saw me following him on the street, he ran to me and we clung to each other a moment before he left with his regiment. The morning was the saddest I've ever known, yet I feel that a part of him…

"The page is torn," Sarah said. " A few lines are missing." She began to read again.

There is no way to know how long he will be gone, or if he will return. We walked beside the still waters of the Battery at dawn. The morning more often than not presents a surface that is gray and slick and plays with the colors of sunrise as the morning dawns. This morning the waters were just so, and Jeremiah's spirit was just as still and quiet as those waters. His last embrace came as the sun peaked the horizon. The carriage came to take him to his regiment, which by now has reached the outskirts of the city, heading towards Camden to engage the Federals. I grieve at his absence and the belief I may never feel his strong arms around me again, or his tender kiss on my lips.

"Whoa," Jack said in a low voice. "More still water, Sarah. And they stayed at The Mills House, albeit an earlier incarnation of the hotel."

"They walked along The Battery and the waters were still

that morning. It fits." She pulled the map out and they studied it. "But the Battery is straight and not curved. The markings on the map could be...I don't know...the cannon."

"The cannon are a later addition," he said. "And there's nothing on the promenade that works either."

"The church was round. I never thought there were so many places that were round or curved." Sarah said matter-of-factly.

"I think we should look over everything once more before heading out again. Let's be sure we're going to the right place this time. And you need to eat something. We can't search effectively if we're starving." He was loath to go out in public again. Every move was an opportunity for arrest.

Sarah pulled a piece of bread from the baguette and topped it with brie. She ate hungrily and drained her coffee.

He did the same and when the food was gone, he felt better. He was happy to see some color had returned to her face and her voice.

They pushed the dishes away and laid everything on the table: the book, the photocopies and the letters.

Sarah poised a pen over her notebook.

"Let's make notes about what we know from these three things—and any of the common elements among them," Sarah said.

"They all talk about still waters."

"True." She jotted that down.

"And we know the statue head is hidden somewhere, buried."

"The author of the diary is Charlotte Beaufain. The writer of the letters is Jeremiah Singleton."

"What about the book?"

Jack picked it up and not seeing the author's name on the

front opened it to the title page.

"Jeremiah was a professor at the college. Her father couldn't have been happy about a professor wooing his young daughter. But Jeremiah was also a soldier."

They flipped through the pages and read the sometimes awkward, but heartfelt text. There were scenes of love, passages of description of the heat of a Charleston summer. It even touched on the early days of the war. The days before war was actually declared.

"They walked hand-in-hand in the heat of the Sunday morning, to the site of the church Mr. Mills helped design and their families had helped build; the church yard in which so many of her family was buried. And they someday would lie side-by-side in this beautiful and somber place of peace. But today his father would go to his final reward under the ancient oaks weeping with graybeard blowing in the soft breeze. They followed the procession along the slate walk that circled the burned-out ruins of the once-proud sanctuary."

"This is a novel, his first book. And he did write earlier in a letter about the novel being an allegory for their lives," Sarah said.

"The church is a quiet, peaceful place, like the water. But it doesn't say anything about the water. The church was first started in the late 1600s, but this is a later building. The one Mills designed burned just before the start of the war and wasn't rebuilt until the 1890s. But the graveyard has remained and endured since the earliest days. It's one of the oldest in the city," Jack said.

"So what does this mean in the scheme of things?" Sarah sank back on the seat sullenly. "What do you think?"

"It makes sense—the novel was special to her and to him."
She set the novel aside and opened another letter.

My dearest sweet Charlotte,
The cold and hunger of the troops has lessened our spirits. We have not eaten in two days and it does not seem likely we will eat today. Your letter talks of the graveyard at our Church. I fear I soon may join the residents. My own dear father is laid to rest there and should I not return alive, I wish that my memory, if not my body, be marked in that quiet place next to my dear parents. Your father and I talked about it as a good place to hide your family's future wealth. He and my father were always saving each other as children at play, and your father's decision to use this family location that will not be disturbed by battle is right and thoughtful. My heart is with you all. My love is with you alone. Be safe in your travels.
Remember me, my Dear Sweet Charlotte,
Jeremiah

"The Circular Church cemetery, Jack!" It's hidden there! Let's go," the enthusiasm he had grown to expect from her had returned. But it was the excitement of the chase…he had a lot to make up for. Or maybe he should do just as she asked. Leave her alone once the project was over. It was just possible he didn't know how to be the right kind of man for her. At least he could be a good work partner. They both believed they had solved the riddle.

He looked up to see a police car pull to the curb in front of the tiny bistro.

Chapter 42

ack knew a way out through the kitchen, took Sarah's hand and led her out of the restaurant. On the sidewalk once again, Sarah scanned the street.

"I don't think we should take my car. They might make the connection to you. We'll leave it here. The Circular Church isn't far."

The Circular Congregational Church had once been inside the city walls that protected early Charleston. It stood today, still an active and inclusive congregation that drew the faithful as well as curious visitors from all over the world. The messages engraved in the cemetery stones and crypts were strong clues to life and the ways people departed the earth back then. The earliest markers were of slate and sported skull and crossbones motifs. Over time that trend morphed into angels. Yellow fever had taken many lives. War, whooping cough, typhoid, childbirth. There were even a couple of pirates laid to rest there. Children who died early waited decades until their parents joined them. Many stones were pre-Revolutionary

War, the church being started in the 1690s. Sarah was fascinated by the old graveyards scattered throughout the city and in some of the outlying areas. She'd visited many of them, mostly to view the sculptures that adorned the plots.

Although some stones had broken and others were illegible, many were in reasonably good shape. The cemetery was well kept and open to visitors. She and Jack would blend in with the other tourists. She wasn't exactly sure what they were looking for, but they had the family names, Singleton and Beaufain. And the map. According to the letter, the statue head was buried with Jeremiah's father. How would they ever be able to retrieve it without desecrating the grave? But first they had to find it. They wandered through the headstones as mosquitoes buzzed in hoards under the live oaks. Crickets bounced over the grass before them. The sun was hot, and the air heavy, oppressive.

"Beaufain," Jack said pointing to the ground at a slab that covered a grave. The date would have preceded Charlotte's birth. It was the only Beaufain in that area. An hour later, they still had not found even one Singleton. Not one. They had covered most of the graveyard and the outcome wasn't feeling nearly as much of a sure thing as it had when they arrived.

"May I help you find someone?" a warbled voice asked behind them. They turned to see a tiny little woman in a straw hat, a flowered shift and sensible shoes. She had a handful of pamphlets.

"Hi. Uh, yes. Actually. We're looking for a Singleton grave. We don't have the first name, but he would have died before or early in the Civil War," he said.

The little woman smiled and squinted up at them through the dappled sunlight. "Oh that would be one of the more recent graves then. I just might be able to help you," she said, her voice, thin and high. Only in Charleston would the Civil war era be considered recent.

She opened a pamphlet and spread out a map of the cemetery on a nearby tomb. She turned it over to find a listing of names of those buried there around them.

"Let's see now. Singleton. Singleton," she said as she traced her finger down the list. "Bingo, dears. Here it is. Singleton. Born 1802. Died 1863. Josiah Singleton."

"Can you show it to us?" Sarah asked, excited that at last they might be making progress. The woman scanned the map and showed them the location. "For a small donation, you can have one of our pamphlets. We use the money for upkeep of the cemetery. It's hard keeping it pretty with so many visitors coming through." Jack reached into his pocket and pulled out a wallet. He handed the woman $10."

"That's very generous, sir," the woman chortled.

"Can you tell us any of the Singleton history?"

"I believe Josiah Singleton died from a wound he received during an early shelling of the city during the recent unpleasantness—known to most folks as the War between the States. Let's see, the war started in 1861 when The Citadel Cadets fired on Fort Sumter. It was a union fort at the time." She pulled a small book from the pocket of her skirt, flipped the pages and read, "Josiah's son was a professor at the College—and a poet or novelist—a writer of some sort. After his father's death, he enlisted and went to war."

Sarah grabbed Jack's arm in the excitement of the moment.

"Jack," she whispered. "We've found it!"

They thanked the woman and followed the path to the Singleton plot. A substantial marble stone sat at one end of the grave. They stood before the weathered marker and read:

Josiah Singleton. Beloved husband of Mamie. Father of Jeremiah and Genevieve. A patriot of the Confederate States of America. He now lies beside the still waters in the care of our Lord.

"Jack, beside the still water!"

The grave perimeter was bordered by cobblestones with a flat stone at the foot engraved with Josiah's regiment name. Next to Josiah was Mamie, his wife.

"This is it, Sarah! This is the right grave. Father of Jeremiah." Jack pulled out the map that had fallen from the diary and every mark lined up, the winding line that would be the path they'd just walked down and the grave itself, with its headstone, footstone and stone border and the image of the map scrap on his phone would be the edge of the church.

Sarah was touched by his excitement. They read the lengthy text describing how Josiah was injured in an early shelling of the city. He had fought bravely for Charleston. But when she looked at the grave to the right of Josiah, she cried out.

"Jack. Look." She grabbed his arm, grief taking its place on her face.

And there, right before them was the end of Charlotte and Jeremiah's love affair.

"It's Jeremiah. He was killed near the end of the war. Look. January, 1865."

They stood there silently mourning the loss of someone who'd been dead for more than 150 years. Yet, it was if they'd just learned of the passing of a friend.

Sarah sighed and looked up at Jack. As handsome as any man she'd ever known. As appealing as she could imagine...

"But now what?" she whispered, shaking herself from romanticizing Jack Chase. A middle-aged couple passed by.

"How do we get the head? How do we even know for sure it's still here?"

"It could have been found decades ago."

Whatever we do, I'm pretty sure it isn't going to happen in the middle of the day. We'll have to dig around the base of the stone—or maybe lift the footstone. It could be under there. We'll have to be careful not to break it—and as soft as marble is, I'm not sure how lucky we'll be."

"You're right. But we have to figure out something." Holt or Atkinson probably know where it is by now, too. And it seems pretty certain he'll stop at nothing to get it."

"Let's go."

"Where to?"

"Anywhere but here. There's nothing more we can do right now. We need a plan."

They followed the curve of the church back to Meeting Street. A city trolley passed.

"Come on," she said grabbing his hand and running toward the corner. "We need transportation!" They would become tourists in their own city, blend in with the throngs roaming the streets.

The trolley made a circle around the city every half hour.

"Let's just ride and think," she said as they settled into a seat near the back. The car was about half full. They were probably the only locals on board. The rhythm of the trolley was relaxing. People came and went. Babies cried, tourists earnestly discussed their next tour, where they would eat dinner. Sarah watched Jack as he poured over his notes. He was committed to bringing the statue head back to the school and replacing it on the torso from which it had been severed. Or was he just as interested in the treasure as Holt and the other man. She could admire his dedication to restoring the statue despite her disappointment with him personally.

Several German tourists boarded the bus and Sarah and Jack slid closer to each other to make room for them on the side bench seat. His leg pressed against hers, impossible to ignore, impossible to acknowledge.

"The letter said the head held their future. The head contains enough to start an entirely new life that mimics what they had before the war."

"Emeralds, gold. People have killed for a whole lot less reason than that." Jack smiled a wistful smile that would melt the hardest heart.

They sat silently for a few minutes swaying to the rhythm of the trolley, their bodies touching, absorbing the motion in tandem, rocking along the city street.

"What if we can't get the head?"

"I have every intention of getting the head. Tonight, Sarah. A crowbar and a shovel should do the trick."

"We're liable to get arrested."

"Well, I figure that's going to happen in my case anyway. Maybe you should go back to your apartment. I'll come to you after I get the head." Jack said the words like a pronouncement.

"Yeah, right. Like I'm going to let you have all the fun."

They both smiled as they passed Hibernian Hall and a knot of tourists soaking in the city's history.

"But for now we need a place to wait, and plan."

Chapter 43

Sarah turned her gaze to the trolley windows and the city beyond as they rolled up East Bay Street. And then she saw him. Holt. Standing on a corner near Queen Street carrying what appeared to be a purple bowling ball bag.

"Jack," she said, grabbing his arm and pointing to the little man on the corner.

"Isn't that Holt?"

"Come on," he said and called out to the driver, "STOP PLEASE! WE NEED TO GET OFF HERE!" the driver smoothly pulled over and they hurried off the trolley. Holt was a block away and had not seen them. He was waiting at a crosswalk for the light to change. They waited until he walked and then followed as far back as they could without losing him.

"Jack, you don't suppose he already has the head in that bag?"

"Doesn't look heavy. And we just left the grave."

"If he gets away…"

"Then we'd best keep up with him," Jack said and flashed that smile of his.

The excitement of the chase had his adrenaline surging and it gleamed in his eyes. They were alive, energized. They crossed the street a block up from where Holt was strolling casually with the bag. He turned the corner and they hurried to follow. They stopped at the edge of the building and peered down the side street. Holt was still walking slowly along. In fact he was the only one walking on this section of Cumberland Street. It would be impossible to follow him without being seen.

"Now what," we'll have to watch from here and move forward as soon as we lose sight of him. He's headed toward Meeting and my guess is toward the Circular Church."

"I hope you're right. At least we'll have him in our sights."

When they looked back, they saw the purple bag disappear around the corner. Holt turned left onto Church Street, just one block from the Circular Church and the grave of Josiah Singleton. How could they stop him without getting arrested themselves?

She looked at the man beside her, handsome, intelligent, driven. Yet, she did not trust him, did not want to trust him. It was nearly 6 p.m. They'd been on the chase all day.

"Let's go," Jack said suddenly, grabbing her hand and pulling her down narrow Chalmers Street. Paintings hung in the windows of several galleries lining the cobblestone lane, and what Jack recognized as a street in the French Quarter art walks. One Friday a month the galleries opened their doors and the public wandered the streets, dipping into small shops, admiring the work, sipping wine provided by the gallery owners, nibbling on local fare like boiled shrimp and fruit. It was always an entertaining way to spend an evening.

But today the street was still, except for the sound of their footsteps as they hurried in the direction Holt had taken. When they neared the spot they last saw him, Jack put out his arm to slow her pace. Holt must have disappeared into one of the galleries. Atelier Petit, would have to be the place. Known for its European acquisitions, it was a favorite of many of the city's art lovers.

Sarah nodded toward a peachy pink house, once a tavern and now a coffee house, across the street almost opposite Atelier Petit.

They found a table near a window, ordered and before long the waiter set cups of espresso on the table and returned with a plate of pastries, cream and sugar.

"Enjoy," he said crisply and with a slight French accent. Sarah had not taken her eyes off the gallery.

"What if we're wrong? What if he's not even in there?"

"He's in there alright. I'd bet everything on it." He laughed. He knew he was doing exactly that, betting everything on it.

He sat silently for a few minutes, sipping the thick coffee, wolfing down a Danish. She picked at a croissant.

And when their eyes met again, he hoped she would try to find common ground with him.

Her hair hung in a dark tangle over her shoulder. He needed her, wanted her touch. For she already had his heart in her hand. She could crush him or embrace him. Since Nadia, he'd allowed no woman any control over him. A sudden rush of fear clenched his core at the realization Sarah held that power and a whole lot more. Did she understand she could decimate him with a look, that she could have him on any terms?

Jack took another sip of the espresso, and his pulse

pounded, not from the rush of caffeine, but from fear of the pain he imagined was to come.

He doodled on the napkin, drew his version of the grave of Josiah and Mamie Singleton and their orientation to the curved wall and paths radiating out from the church. Putting the image to paper in his own hand helped him think. He sketched the body length grave, the head and footstones. Then he added the marble vases mounted in the ground at the head of each, vases that were empty, waiting for flowers that no longer came as the people who loved them had also died, all their love passing into oblivion. It suddenly seemed overwhelmingly sad. He continued to draw, adding detail after detail.

"Does this look right?"

"I think so. Wait. Let's compare." She pulled the baggie with the scrap of map from her purse and handed it to Jack. He laid it next to his phone image and his own rendering. The similarities were spot on.

"What are these marks?"

He studied his drawing. Something was missing. The cobblestones that bordered the grave. He quickly added them in and again compared his drawing to the crude map.

"There's a mark here. This stone. Near the head of Josiah's grave. OH MY GOD, Jack! Do you see what I see?"

"Sarah, we need a shovel."

"I'm going to scoot into the ladies room before we go. We are going aren't we?"

"You better believe it."

He called the waiter over as Sarah disappeared into the restroom. "Do you know where I could find a shovel near here?"

"A shovel Monsieur?"

"Yes, something to dig with. For a garden? Do you know where I could get something like that?"

"I have a shovel sir, behind the shop. But it is not a very good one."

"I'll buy it from you. How much?"

"It is a very poor shovel. You are welcome to use it."

Jack dropped a twenty on the table. "Is that enough?"

"Of course it is more than enough. Please, you take it. Here, I will show you."

Sarah was on her way back to the table. Jack pointed to the waiter, "Be right back."

He followed the waiter outside, and found the shovel leaning against the back wall near a storage shed. It was old, but would certainly serve their purpose. They would forget Holt and go right away to the cemetery. The head was not buried completely. It was there in plain view. And he and Sarah would have it before the hour was out.

He grabbed the shovel, inspected it briefly and hurried back down the garden path to Sarah and the front of the store. He propped the shovel near the door and went inside. Sarah was not at the table.

"Sir? Where is the lady?"

"Perhaps the ladies room, I believe."

Jack settled back into his chair. She shouldn't have left her post. She should know better than that. He pulled a twenty dollar bill from his wallet and dropped it on the table next to the one he'd already left for the shovel. A brilliant sunset faded into a gray blue pall over the city. The gaslights, nearly invisible during the day, flickered into existence as night closed in. Jack eyed the gallery. Then cast a glance back at the ladies room.

Sarah wouldn't have left her post. And then he saw the

napkin on the floor and Sarah's note.

Following Holt, it said in a loose scrawl. Holt had left the gallery and Sarah had gone after him. *Damn.* He pocketed the napkin, ran out the door, grabbed the shovel and headed down the street. In the closing light, he thought he saw two forms, one further away on the opposite side of the street, the other a little closer, and both making their way down Chalmers toward Meeting Street.

He hoped it was Sarah and Holt.

Chapter 44

Jack tried to cover the space between him and Sarah as quickly as he could without getting Holt's attention. The dark was good cover, but it also made it difficult to see ahead. Was Sarah okay?

He ran as quietly as he could, occasionally stopping to assess what was happening up ahead. But the two people were still moving steadily forward. And Jack followed, quickly, stealthily until the form closest to him, the one he hoped was Sarah, passed by the flickering gas street lamps and he was relieved to see that it was. He started to call quietly, but held back, closed more ground as he ran silently forward.

When the assault came Jack was on the ground before he could even cry out, crashed onto his back, his shovel rattling metallically on the flagstone walk. The dark form again lunged at him.

Sat on him.

Barked at him.

"Jethro, get off that man," a deeply Charleston lady accent

said lazily. The dog was by now licking Jack's face.

"Jethro, bad boy. You okay," the woman laughed, offering him a hand up. Jack got to his feet.

"I'm fine. Just a little surprised," he said as he regained his balance and tried to calm his racing pulse.

"Jethro's just a puppy, but he's a big baby with lots of enthusiasm." She put Jethro back in the gate. The huge Great Dane puppy stood against the gate, stretched to a height of six feet or better.

"I'm fine. Gotta go," he said, waving off her protests, pushing away her solicitous clutching hands, and grabbing up his shovel.

"I can get you some lemonade? What you doin' with that shovel?" her voice trailed off behind him as he rushed to regain the ground he'd lost. The dark had closed in completely eliminating any sense of motion up ahead, the forms absorbed into the inky night. The gaslights stood further apart on this section of the street. He waited anxiously for Sarah to arrive at the next light. Where was she?

He stood still, looking ahead, squinting into the dark, trying to see anything—something that would let him know he was on the right track and that Sarah was just ahead. But he saw nothing. No movement on either side of the street. *Where did they go?*

He sprinted forward, caution be damned. He had to find her. *If something were to happen to her…*

At a small parking area, he looked for any sign they were near, and saw nothing. Nothing! He cleared the open area and continued on Chalmers toward Meeting. He was only two blocks from the graveyard. Sarah must have followed Holt there. He prayed Holt had not discovered her. *Please stay safe, Sarah. Please, be careful* his heart beat out the words as he retraced the steps they'd made together earlier that day. It'd been daylight then; now it was the darkest of nights, a new moon, and what had seemed simple in the daylight was completely different in the dark.

He walked through the narrow side street gate into the churchyard, keeping to the shadows. He searched the blackness cast by the building, cast in silhouette by the lights that flanked the sanctuary's arched double doors. There was no sign of Sarah or Holt. He half hoped to see a flashlight amid the gravestones. But nothing.

Lights beamed upward on the front and roof of the church making the dark of the cemetery impenetrable. The deep shadows hid the centuries-old trees, the moss hanging over cracked and weathered tombs and marble monuments.

A raised slate pathway wound through gravesites that had been there nearly 400 years and towards the Singleton plot. Jack stood perfectly still for several minutes, hoping for a sign that someone else might be in the cemetery. His wait was met with solemn silence but his eyes began to adjust.

He crept forward, avoiding a slim beam of light that penetrated from the front of the church, and kept to the packed grass near the wrought iron and brick fence. He skirted close to trees and the taller monuments marking lives long gone. Moss-covered brick leaked out an earthy scent while out in the real world a car horn honked, and a man yelled at a pedestrian to stop taking photos from the middle of the street.

Jack made his way toward the back, holding the shovel like a baseball bat ready to defend himself—and Sarah too if he ever found her.

Fingers scraped over the top of his head. "Damn!" he whispered, swung around and flailed the shovel in an arc, and attacked the moss hanging from a low limb. He smiled nervously to himself and said a soundless "Damn!" again. He took a deep breath and refocused. Hands sweating, clothes suddenly feeling too tight.

The tombstones gathered the ambient light to glow an eerie gray-green, like ghosts themselves, waiting there in the dark to live again. Jack felt a little lightheaded, and leaned against a live oak, hidden behind a drooping branch. *What the hell was he doing in a graveyard in the dark? Had he lost his mind? Get a grip, Jack.*

How come it always seemed so stupid when people in movies did it and now, for some unfathomable reason, tonight, it didn't seem stupid at all. *Scary as hell. But not stupid.* He had a mission. He had to find Sarah, and together they would find the statue's head. He scanned the cemetery again and leaned back into the shadows.

A car passed out on the street, radio full throttle, bleating out "Carolina Girl." Beach music. Could it have been less than a week that Sarah walked in on him in mid-spin singing to himself, dancing in the ceramics room? It seemed like months.

The music faded and he crept out of the shadows and back onto the path. A motion to his side nearly gave him a heart attack. He swung the shovel, metal nearly hitting stone. Jack looked, but it was only a toad hopping across a cracked gravestone. He slumped, took a breath, looked around to be sure no one had seen or heard him thrashing around. The street noise of a passing bus had camouflaged the noise.

Really embarrassed, he moved on down the path. He would go to the grave, remove the cobble he believed to be the statue's head and then what? He had to find Sarah. That would be pretty hard to do if he was toting the equivalent of a bowling ball around—minus the finger holes even. No, he had to be sure Sarah was safe before he retrieved the head. Hell. Holt could be digging the head up while he stood here agonizing.

Movement once again caught his attention, and he slipped into shadow behind a monument. Sounds of someone digging froze him momentarily. Then adrenaline took over, drawing him toward the Singleton plot, shovel ready for action. And there was the source of the noise: Holt. Digging. Holt had a small penlight clutched in lips and trained on the grave. It was very faint, but enough to illuminate the action. Holt was digging near the foot of the graves. Jack watched silently, searching the surrounding trees and bushes for any sign of Sarah. And then, in the dark, there she was, on the far side of the park, crouching behind a tombstone, barely visible. At first he thought he was looking at one of the obelisks dotting the graveyard. But then the statue moved, ever so slightly, and he was sure it was Sarah. They were both watching. But what to do now? He didn't want to startle Holt. He might have a gun. He wouldn't take that kind of chance with Sarah so close.

Holt threw a large round cobble to the side, cursing his frustration.

As soon as Holt started digging again, Jack inched closer, deciding to let Holt dig to his heart's content. Maybe Holt would give up and leave. Or maybe he would find the head and save them all the trouble.

He saw Sarah move again. At least he could see she was safe for now. He drew a deep breath, released it slowly. It was the first time he'd taken a real breath since he'd returned to the coffee shop and found Sarah missing.

And then Holt lifted a stone, held it up and explored it with his penlight.

Jack watched, entranced as Holt carefully slipped the

statue head into the bowling bag, turned, and walked quickly down the side path. Sarah fell in discreetly behind him, a good 20 yards away.

Jack slipped across the path, held the shovel in baseball bat position, stepped over the stones Holt had dug up and discarded in his search for the statue head. He had to catch up to Sarah without alerting Holt he was being pursued. Sarah and Holt disappeared behind a curve in the path. By the time Jack got to the place where he lost sight of them, he knew the flash of motion on the street meant Sarah had cleared the gate and was now back on the street following Holt.

Jack ran full out to the gate. There was no one to hide from now. Only the dead were witness to his desperation to catch up to Sarah and Holt. He burst onto the sidewalk, nearly head-on into a couple of beat police.

"Can I help you, sir?" the first policeman asked sternly.

"No, thanks. I'm fine." Jack tried to make the shovel less huge, less menacing.

"We've had a report from the church of some possible vandalism in the graveyard," the policeman said, eyeing the shovel up and down. "You want to tell us what you're doing with that shovel Mr.—I didn't catch your name."

"Jenkins. Joe Jenkins."

"May I see your identification, please," the second officer asked.

"Uhh, I lost my wallet. I might have left it at home."

"Doing a little digging tonight are we?"

"There was a man, he ran out ahead of me. He was digging up a grave. This is his shovel," Jack said, seizing on the idea and going with it. "I was chasing him. You must have seen him." Jack tried to stay calm.

"Hey Carl, that guy that nearly knocked us down." They

both looked down the street in the direction that Holt had disappeared.

"I'll show you where he was digging," he said suddenly.

"Let's drop the shovel, sir," the first officer said.

Jack propped it against the cemetery wall. He led the way down the path he'd just traveled, winding back into the dark graveyard, the officers casting their flashlights forward to light the way.

He had to make a decision. It's over here, he called over his shoulder and bounded ahead as if to show the policemen the location of the digging. He had to get away. It wouldn't take long before they'd know his name was Jack Chase and he was a wanted man. No doubt they'd think he'd beaten Rachel and trashed her office. He had to find out where Sarah had gone. He couldn't take a chance something would happen to her because of him.

"Over here," he called again. As the officers moved forward, he ducked behind a tree, then zig-zagged over to the monument he'd stood behind to watch Holt. He moved on to the tree where he'd rested, then back to the front gate. He grabbed the shovel as the officers shouted for him to stop, but they couldn't see him. He slipped onto the street, ran to the corner and rounded onto Chalmers, retracing his earlier steps.

And on the next corner was his out. A bike parked outside a restaurant. He hopped on it and disappeared back down Chalmers, bumping over uneven sidewalk slates, but hanging on and making progress. *Where are you Sarah?*

The police had given up the chase and were no doubt calling in reinforcements at this point.

Jack's chest pounded with the exertion. He was approaching the coffee house they'd sat in earlier watching for Holt. He didn't even know where to start the search for Sarah.

She was okay. She had to be. She was smart and he'd seen her leave the graveyard under her own power.

He pulled into the small, gated courtyard that flanked the coffee shop. He'd regroup here. It was closed now, but a small light shown from the doorway as he wheeled the stolen bike against the wall. He stood at the building's corner, hidden from the street. He needed to think.

A cat padded softly past him and he smiled.

A sound, a cry, maybe a cat, across the street at Atelier Petit. Jack glanced up and saw, not another cat, but movement across the street. When a door slammed and lights came on in the shop he leaned forward and pushed the branches of the azalea bush aside to clear his view. Across the street, inside the gallery, stood Sarah—her arms pulled tight behind her back—wide-eyed, defiant and scared.

And next to her, also tied up—was Holt. Another man was talking, waving his arms, an orator with an audience of two. No. Make that four. Sitting on a pedestal in front of Sarah was a statue head. Covered in dirt. Leaning against an interior wall was the blond man. When the unknown orator turned, he was no longer unknown. It was Atkinson.

Grabbing the shovel Jack ran silently across to the gallery and carefully stood on tiptoe to look in the window.

Chapter 45

Sarah's hands, bound tight with heavy cord, pulsed near numbness. Heart racing, breathing too fast. She needed to regain her composure. A clear head was essential if she had any hope of getting away. She glanced at Holt who appeared to be unconscious. The huge blond man had hit him hard.

She couldn't believe she was here, the prisoner of Atkinson. Her arms ached, her head hurt, her lungs struggled for air. Where was Jack when she needed him? Seemed like he'd been all over the place and now he was nowhere. Nowhere. Would he think to look for her here? Was that Jack she'd seen in the cemetery? She couldn't be sure, but it could have been. Or it could have been a lingering tourist. *Please let that have been Jack.*

Atkinson paced back and forth, shouting, acting really nuts as he told her about the importance of the statue's head. He ranted about the college. About Craig Duncan. Something about Holt and his grandmother and the diary. What possible connection could Holt's *grandmother* have to the diary?

And the head? There it stood on a pedestal in the middle of the room. Dirt hung around the hairline like a laurel on Caesar's head. Despite the finely carved features and the musing look on the statue's face, it was otherwise ordinary.

Portraits hung on the walls, their subjects watching skeptically as Atkinson continued to rant. The blond man leaned in the corner, scraping under his nails with a toothpick. In his waistband stood a large hunting knife much like the one her father carried. The blond giant looked up occasionally, listening half-heartedly, apparently bored with the whole thing. But she knew him now to be violent and the kind who enjoyed inflicting pain on others. He was capable of seriously hurting her without a thought. He had cut one throat and now she believed he had intended to cut Rachel's as well. Only Jack's arrival at Rachel's had stopped him from completing his grisly task.

The blond giant had come up behind her as she followed Holt to the gallery. Before she knew anything was wrong, he'd grabbed her, wrapped one arm tight around her waist and pulled her back against him. She remembered a tiny little cry escaped her before his hammy hand clamped over her mouth. She wasn't even sure the sounds had come from her. Blondie had half-dragged her into the studio.

Atkinson paced, sporting an amused look.

"So you didn't know anything about a diary," he said smugly, sneering at her as he continued back and forth across the gallery, hands behind his back, lecturing. While Atkinson attempted to talk them to death, the blond killer roughly checked her bound hands.

So, here she was with a violent blond body builder, a weird little man whose motives had something to do with his grandmother and the contractor in charge of the renovation who apparently would go to almost any length to get what he wanted and she, a woman following clues to the end. She just hoped it wasn't the end of her. She needed Jack. Where was he? She'd made a split-second decision to follow Holt and left before Jack returned from behind the coffee shop with the shovel.

That seemed hours ago but could only have been 20 or 30 minutes at most. Her arms and hands alternated between pain and numbness. And fear. Fear, ready to boil over, was making her incapable of thought. But one crazy person in the room was enough, and it was for sure Atkinson was crazy. That fact was frighteningly plain right now as he ranted on about artifacts and people who didn't appreciate their importance. That items like this should belong to people who knew how to appreciate them—someone like him—someone who could use the treasure to enjoy life the way it should be enjoyed.

Blondie returned to his manicure, glancing up at Atkinson every now and again.

She worked her hands against the ropes, tried to loosen the knot, but the rough rope tore at her hands. She fingered it, gripped one round section between a forefinger and thumb and pulled. *Ouch. Damn.* Her fingernail tore to the quick. Tears sprang to her eyes in her effort not to show her pain. *Damn.* She could do this. She had to do this. She picked at the rope again. The pain. The wet pain. She knew now that her finger was bleeding, wetting the rope. Would it make the knot easier to slip? She let the twine rip her nail a little more. Oh God it hurt. She took a shallow breath, bit her lip. But the blood dripped a little more and the knot eased a little bit. Hope was quickly replacing fear as the dominant emotion.

When the blond dude came to stand in front of her, she

had nearly loosened her bonds and was having to work very hard to hold onto the length of rope so they would not recognize her deceit. Atkinson's back was to her. And there in the middle of the room the statue watched.

Chapter 46

Jack heard another voice in the room—quiet, low, menacing. Someone walked between Atkinson and the window. The blond man from the pier.

An argument was in progress on the other side of the window. Jack hugged his back to the wall, making his way into the side courtyard to see if there was another entrance. Steep stone steps, nearly invisible against a vine-covered wall, led to a second floor landing. He had to give it a try. And he had to let the police know what was going on. He did a quick search on his phone, found the number he believed to be the police department, and asked for Mallory.

"Please leave a message…" Jack quickly left the name of the gallery, his name and a cryptic, "Help needed" was the only message he had time for when he heard shouting from the gallery. He put the phone on silent and slipped it back into his pocket.

With his shovel he stepped tentatively up the first few steps, stopped and listened, then took the last five to the landing and a dark wood door with a leaded glass window.

His hand trembled as he reached for the doorknob. In the distance, a couple laughed and music wafted up to him from a nearby house. Chicken grilling nearby smelled like heaven. *Focus, Jack.*

He withdrew his hand, blew out a breath, shook his hand, repositioned the shovel, and tried again. When the doorknob turned easily, he silently did the dance of joy. Within a second he stood on the dark upper floor of the old house. Voices filtered up from downstairs. A streetlight flickered its glow into the room, showing the wide planks of antique pine floors, the kind of floors that scream and creak when walked on.

Jack leaned over and gently laid the shovel down. Even that small motion caused the board beneath his feet to groan ever so quietly. And he had to cross a room full of these old boards. He could just make out a hallway and what appeared to be a banister that could signal stairs to the gallery.

He took a deep breath and sat down on the floor. Then as quietly as he'd laid down the shovel, he spread out his legs in a wide V, picked up the shovel and laid it across the tops of his thighs and scooted very slowly forward. If he could spread out his weight and not pressure any particular board, he might make it to the other side without alerting Atkinson. He pushed along, an inch at a time, making progress, silently moving toward the stairs—and Sarah.

The voices sounded stronger as he approached the hallway. Atkinson's voice was controlled, almost too controlled. The other voice was irritated, menacing.

"Let me finish them off," the blond giant said. "I'm tired of this—and you've got what we came for."

"NO!" Atkinson raged at the man. We are not, do you hear me, not, getting rid of them here."

Jack scooted forward, closer, closer.

A door slammed and footsteps pounded up the stairs toward him.

He scrunched up against the wall, pulled his legs in and gripped the shovel handle. The heard him. They must have. Should he go for it? Sarah was downstairs, bound, unable to help herself. The footsteps gained the top landing and turned off the other way. A light flipped on. The guy was taking a leak. It was the blond guy.

He had to make a move. He lifted the shovel and slipped the handle end into the hallway across the head of the stairs. If blondie turned the bathroom light off, he would never see the shovel.

The toilet flushed and Jack braced for whatever was to come. Blondie came out of the bathroom—and left the light on! Damn.

Just before he reached the head of the stairs, he turned and went back to the bathroom and flipped off the lights.

Yes!

Blondie rounded the banister, caught his foot on the shovel handle and for a few seconds seemed to hang in mid-air groping for the banister, pin-wheeling his arms in a desperate act of levitation.

The shovel chased him into the air, turned end up and came to a crashing blow on Blondie's head eliciting an aerial howl. There was way more racket than Jack had imagined. Bumping, crashing, metallic banging of the shovel against the wall, screams and howls from Blondie.

Jack was on his feet, following the tumbling big guy down the steps, praying that his own presence would be camouflaged by the racket.

He leapt over the prostrate and semi-conscious man and

took the knife from his belt and grabbed the shovel that now rested against the gallery door. The pontificating in the next room had gone silent. Silence was quickly followed by orders being barked, and footsteps heading to the door. Jack backed against the wall, knife, now in his waistband, shovel ready for action. And when the door opened and Atkinson emerged, Jack let loose with a wide swing that brought the shovel blade in direct contact with Atkinson's chest.

The sound of air rushing out of the orator was stunning in its loudness. Atkinson slumped to the floor, struggling to bring air back into his lungs. Jack stood stock still for about three beats, then shoved a writhing Atkinson aside so he could get to Sarah. She was strangely silent.

Jack cleared the door and there she was, tied up to a narrow pillar near the back of the room. When she saw him she cried out, "JACK!"

"SARAH!" He ran to her, brushing the hair from her face with both hands, frantically assessing her. "My God, are you okay?"

"Help me untie this. Quickly!" She said, wrestling with the remainder of the rope binding her. Jack went behind the pole and tried to loosen the last knot and made it tighter. He felt like a bumbling halfwit. Finally he got hold of the right piece of rope and the knot slid apart.

"JACK!" Sarah called out. He looked up from his work to get a face full of shovel.

"Take that you son of a bitch," blondie yelled at Jack and kicked at him as he fell, grabbing at air, to the floor.

"Jack! Jack!" Sarah screamed, forcing him to hang on to an edge of consciousness.

He clutched at the floor and spat out the salty wash of blood that flooded his mouth. Jack curled up in a ball before puling himself up, dodging the second swing of the shovel and lurching for blondie's legs, grabbing him around the knees and twisting him to the ground. On the way down the blond giant reached out to grab something to break his fall. What his hand latched onto was the statue head.

Jack saw it tumble from the pedestal, end-over-end it crashed to the pine floor. When it hit, it landed with the sound of a more than a century of silence breaking loose and falling apart.

"Noooo!" Sarah cried an anguished cry as she watched the head fall. Jack followed her gaze and saw the head hit, seeing the piece of ancient art crack in two.

Jack's fury burst forth and he launched another assault on the blond man, slugging him as he tried to get up. Jack grabbed him by the neck of his shirt and hit him one more time and then let him drop to the floor.

He turned back to Sarah who was shaking circulation back into her hands, blood dripping from her torn fingernail.

"You're bleeding! Oh my God! Are you okay?" he asked.

"I broke a nail," she said weakly, a trembling smile making its way to her lips. She scanned the room. "Where's Atkinson?"

The words had no sooner left her mouth than racket in the back hallway caused both of them to turn and Jack to run in the direction of the noise.

"Stop! Charleston PD!" a man shouted on the side patio. Fast footsteps ran toward the gallery. Atkinson nearly knocked Jack down in his haste to get away from the police officers who by now had entered the hallway, guns drawn and ready-for-battle looks on their faces.

Jack grabbed the retreating Atkinson from behind, holding him at the shoulders in a giant bear hug and refusing to give an inch as Atkinson flailed and kicked in vain. Within seconds the policemen were in the room, handcuffing Atkinson, then checking out the blond giant. After determining blondie's injuries were minimal, they handcuffed him, too. Jack was next.

"But officers!" Sarah hollered. "He's not one of the bad guys! He's not."

The officer looked at him.

"Aren't you the same guy who ran from us at the cemetery a little while ago?"

"Yes sir, but as you can see, I was rescuing a beautiful lady in distress." Jack made a halfhearted smile, eyebrows raised.

"It's true, officer. He…he saved my life. If he hadn't come along I think they planned to kill me. And Mr. Holt."

"We'll sort this out at headquarters," the policeman said, checking the handcuffs digging into Jack's wrists. "You okay, Miss?"

"I'm fine. Now," she said. The officer walked to the door and started directing the scene.

Jack tried to adjust his arms to be more comfortable. It was a futile effort. He looked at Sarah. He wanted to hold her. That would be the best feeling in the world. His wrists ached. She came to him and kissed his cheek.

"Sarah," he whispered into her hair. "Thank God you're safe."

"And you?" she asked, lifting her face to his, a smile hiding just behind her concern. And for the first time he knew that there was hope for him.

"I will be. I'm sure I will be."

Chapter 47

The officers dealing with Atkinson and the blond, had their backs to Sarah and Jack. Another officer was trying to rouse Holt who was still tied to the pillar and mostly unconscious.

"Sarah," Jack directed her gaze with his eyes as he looked toward the broken statue. Her smile was gone now as she scoured the floor for the bowling bag and found it shoved against the far corner, hidden just behind a small table.

She grabbed it up and went to the broken statue hiding near the edge of the pedestal. Her hand brushed Jack's leg as she gathered the two pieces into the purple satchel. No jewels or gold were visible. Had they been wrong? The officer still had his back to them as he continued to oversee the proceedings on the patio. It was pretty obvious they didn't consider Jack much of a villain since he was the one who had called for help.

Atkinson and the blond man were being read their rights. The words seemed to pulse like bad lyrics to her hammering heartbeat. Speed was essential.

As Sarah pulled the zipper closed on the bag, Officer Abby Owens entered the room.

"You okay?"

"Fine, officer," Sarah said, holding the bag slightly behind her as if it were a purse. It could have been. It was purple after all. She didn't think anyone had noticed the bag earlier.

"We're going to need you down at the station for a statement, Miss Singleton."

"Of course," she nodded. "Officer, Jack is the hero here. He isn't part of what happened to me, other than to rescue me."

"Mr. Chase. We meet again," Officer Owens said. "Seems there's a warrant out for your arrest in another matter."

Det. Skeet Mallory joined the scene, looking as rumpled as usual.

"Ms. Singleton. Looks like you've had a difficult evening."

"I know I need to come down to the station for a statement. May I go home and get cleaned up first. It's been kind of an ordeal," Sarah said in a super girly-girl voice that Jack, quite frankly, had never heard pass her lips. It was impressive. She held her torn finger up for the officer's inspection.

"Oooh, that's nasty," he said. "Do you want to go by the emergency room?"

"I'll be fine if I can have a shower and grab a bandage."

"Sure Miss Singleton. I'll get an officer to drive you home," he said in a most sincere, gentlemanly voice. The policeman didn't notice the bag.

Within minutes Sarah was home pulling the statue pieces from the bowling bag to assess the damage.

The two halves were each intact. She lifted the right half and placed it on the table. A crack started at the top right and broke down one side of the nose and down past the lips.

She sat and stared at it, mesmerized by the disfigured face. The cracked away side of both pieces was caked with dried mud and moss.

"Seems like I've been searching for this my whole life," Sarah whispered to herself and at the same time knowing it had been only a few days. An important few days.

Sarah went into the kitchen and got a wet paper towel and started cleaning the decades of graveyard debris from the face. She dabbed away at the dirt the way a mother would the face of her child.

And when the interior surface was finally clean, and the light from the kitchen reflected off the surface, she pulled up a chair and sat down, mesmerized by what was there.

"Oh my. Oh," she said more quietly than she had ever uttered true words.

Jack was right—she wanted to tell him so. Now. She ran through a quick shower, bandaged her hand and fled to the police station.

Chapter 48

Jack looked like a child sitting in the principal's office waiting for punishment. He sat alone at the same table they'd sat at together earlier in the day.

She tapped on the window. He looked up and smiled a sweet, almost sad, smile. He shrugged his shoulders, a "what's a guy to do?" kind of look.

"Miss Singleton," Skeet Mallory said as he walked down the hall toward her.

"Skeet. Hi. I gave my statement to the officer. He said Jack could go soon."

"He sure can. Seems the earlier complaint against him has been withdrawn."

"Thanks, Skeet."

Chapter 49

Jack was moved by the gentleness with which Sarah cared for the broken statue. When she turned and saw him looking at her, he looked away, a little embarrassed by his transparency.

He inspected the front of the left half before turning it over to inspect the broken edge.

"This is beautiful, Sarah!" he whispered hoarsely, intensely. His cheek had a bad cut that had been stitched and sported butterfly bandages.

"Just look at this!" He held the piece out for her inspection. The inside was lined with gold. Soft, pure gold. She looked at the other half of the head and began to clean it. The break was covered in slimy dirt, the kind that would have made its way into a fissure over many years, a fine sediment that had collected in a crack that must have opened up decades earlier. The fall from the pedestal this evening had simply ripped the pieces apart that were already damaged. When Holt dug it up, the head was probably just barely in one piece.

Again she rubbed gently at the rough broken section. As she did, the gold interior of this half was also revealed. Embedded in the gold were what appeared to be dozens of jewels—emeralds, rubies, sapphires and what could have been diamonds.

"It truly is a treasure, Jack."

"So it seems," he said. "It's even more fabulous than we imagined. No wonder Atkinson was so keen on getting the head. All that talk about the integrity of the college and the renovation was just as much bullshit as we thought it was…even more so."

"What are we going to do with it?" she asked.

"That's up to you."

"No, it's up to the college."

"I'm not so sure about that. It legally might go to the Beaufain family."

"Or the Singletons," he said, and poked her playfully in the ribs.

"Different Singletons," she said plainly.

"You don't know that. After all, the last thing we read was the Beaufain's plan for moving to the hills of North Carolina to wait out the war. And Jeremiah could have gone looking for her," Jack said.

"Not likely. Remember the graveyard. Jeremiah was buried there with his parents. He died in 1865 of wounds suffered in the war. It's not likely he and Charlotte ever saw each other again," Sarah said sadly. She looked up at Jack. "When they said goodbye that morning on the Battery, I believe she knew it could be the last time they kissed."

"And it probably was."

"We'll do some research and see what turns up. I'm not sure what the law is on that sort of thing, but seems like it's only fair it should go back to the family—if they can be found," Sarah said a little wistfully. "Do you suppose this is a second head, or do you think it was originally of gold...oh Jack. You don't suppose the whole statue is gold, do you?"

"Not the whole statue." He didn't look at her, but the corners of his mouth crimped upwards. His grin was unmistakable, even in profile. "I've explored it thoroughly. I had some digital imaging done, and a quarter-inch core was drilled, along with weight-analysis for the whole piece. Our best guess is there's a cavity about three inches wide, three feet long filled with gold."

They both sat quietly for a few minutes, side-by-side, looking straight ahead, both smiling.

"Sarah?"

"Hmmm?"

He didn't say anything, forcing her to turn and look at him. "Yes?"

"May I hold your hand?"

Again, silence.

She looked away, fingered the partial head of the statue.

She didn't move away from him, but stayed as they had been, facing the statue. He would swear he could feel their heartbeats pulsing together.

She locked her gaze to his, courageously daring him to look away. He summoned his soul to be brave and held steady, refusing to shrink away from her challenge. His body rose to the moment. When she reached for his hand and kissed his palm, he was a goner. His breath quickened, though he tried to hide it. His blood pounded in his head, forcing the pulse lower and lower until his whole body seemed to have established a rhythm that surely she could hear.

Without looking at him, she took his hand and held it in

her lap.

This was the chance he'd hoped for. This was new territory for him. Territory he was ready to explore.

He leaned toward her. It was a tentative kiss, pristine, but with promise. She led him to the spiral staircase

"We have something here, Jack."

He nodded, unable to speak. He was afraid of the emotion this moment had dredged up, yet he was braver than he'd ever been. He would not run from this, he would not make a joke of it or treat it cheaply. He would let her lead him to the place they should go. She would be his guide to what would happen next. His surrender to Sarah Singleton was complete. He was hers to do with as she wanted.

Chapter 50

The wind had picked up and a chill traced across Sarah's shoulders. She watched Jack, his eyes closed, breathing deeply, his head on her chest. She tickled the back of his neck, fingered the chain on his neck. He looked up at her with a tenderness she'd never known.

"Tell me about this. You always have it on."

He stiffened slightly, then relaxed.

"My mother gave it to me a long time ago. I was fourteen. She told me it was important. That I should keep it with me always."

"Do you know why?"

He shook his head. "She said something about it being part of my heritage." He shrugged. "She never said more and I never asked."

"Let's go inside," she said quietly.

"Sounds good to me," he said, pushing against her.

"I mean inside the apartment," she said, grinning at him, poking his chest with her finger.

That night as they slept, she dreamed of swirling green ashes ball gowns, and handsome men with golden faces.

Chapter 51

Morning dawned to the sound of pounding. Someone was at the door.

Sarah pulled on her bathrobe and opened the door to find Detective Skeet Mallory holding that day's newspaper and a big smile on his face.

"You made the front page—again," he said, handing it to her.

"Thanks," she said, taking the folded paper and spreading it on the table. "Wow," she said as she looked at the rather elaborate story situated just above the fold, with a photo of the two men being handcuffed and taken into custody. The story was good, solid. Dan's photos told the a story.

Sarah glanced back toward the bedroom where Jack was still sleeping and towards the table where the statue's head stood covered by a tablecloth she'd thrown over it last night.

"What about Holt?" she asked.

"Holt's in the hospital with minor injuries and some heart issues from all the stress."

"Speaking of Holt, he asked me to give this to you. Looks like the diary you said had been stolen from you," Mallory said, handing her a diary that was nearly identical to the one that had been stolen. "It's not actually part of the investigation so I might as well return it to you for the college. Or is there someone else I should give it to?"

"No. I'm happy to have it, Skeet."

"The charges against Atkinson and the blond dude will be at the very least, assault and kidnapping. And it looks like murder. Craig Duncan. Poor kid. Made a bad choice getting mixed up in this."

"Do you know what they were after?"

"Some letter with directions to a buried treasure. Kid was trying to make a little extra money so he could come back to college next year." Skeet said, shaking his head at the sadness of it all.

"Kid had a letter he found in a book while doing research for the renovation. Told Atkinson about it. Told him he'd give it to him for a price, $10,000. Otherwise Duncan planned to turn it over to you, Miss Singleton."

"To me?"

"Atkinson hired blondie to get it from Duncan—didn't want the kid killed, but the blond maniac...well, subtleties aren't part of his bag of tricks."

"But why kill Craig?"

"The guy is not as stupid as he looks. Realized there was a substantial treasure. My guess is he'd've killed Atkinson and taken the whole lot if you two hadn't intervened."

Sarah, glanced toward the table. She wasn't ready to tell the police about the treasure. Not yet.

"The blond dude followed Duncan...and finally saw his chance to get the letter with no questions asked. A sociopath.

No conscience at all. A real tool."

"We found the letter in Atkinson's possession. Talked about where to find the treasure. My guys are checking it out now."

She started to tell Mallory the diary wasn't the one that was stolen, but thought better of it. This must be the one Holt had referred to when he said he'd discovered a subsequent diary. And where was the diary she had found?

She held the book to her chest, eager for him to leave so she could find out what happened to Charlotte—and sadly she already knew what Jeremiah's fate had been.

She crawled back into bed and shook Jack awake.

"Look what I've got," she whispered. He opened an eye to see the diary.

"It's the diary," he groaned.

"Not *the* diary. *A* diary."

Jack sat up and ran his hands through his hair.

"Detective Mallory just brought it by. Holt's diary. The one Holt said was written after Charlotte and her family left Charleston during the war."

She turned to the front page. In a familiar hand, was the name, Charlotte Beaufain. But this time there was the additional name, Singleton.

"She took the name Singleton. In her heart they were married," Sarah said.

"I understand that...now..." Jack said, tracing his finger down the ridge of her nose.

Sarah flipped through the pages, and began reading on a page marked with a rose petal.

I felt our baby moving inside of me today. I long for the day when you will be here with us, me and our child, holding us and protecting us from the world.

"Jack! She was pregnant." Sarah flipped through a few more.

My heart has shattered. My dear father has died in an accident as he was carrying a wagon loaded with supplies for our troops. The horses became spooked and the wagon overturned before he got off our mountain.

"Oh, Jack," Sarah said sadly.
"Poor Charlotte."
She read on.

The baby is late. Mother is concerned, but there is no doctor. He left to help our wounded troops, for which I am grateful. Mother's health is declining since Father's death. I am afraid of being alone without my parents and without my dear Jeremiah. Our baby consumes my every thought.

Four pages further on Mrs. Beaufain's fate unfolded.

Mother was laid to rest today beside Father. I am alone in the world, although the neighbors who live some distance from here say they will look in on me and our sweet child growing and kicking inside me. I do not know how I will deliver our child alone, but I have no one else to help me. It is possible that Amalie, the neighbor lady, will come and stay with me when my time draws nearer.

"I can't imagine how frightened she must have been," Sarah whispered.

I've named our baby Jared. He is a beautiful boy, sweet of nature and strong. He reminds me of my dear Jeremiah. I delivered the child by myself, although Amalie arrived soon after and helped me to care for him for several days. My strength has not returned, but Amalie assures me it will. I must give myself time, but my will is shaky when I think of how much has been lost, and how much I miss Jeremiah.

"She misses him so much. I can't even imagine the hell she was going through, there all alone." When Sarah turned the page, the writing had changed. It was less elegant, almost childlike. Not an educated hand.

I am writing this for the child whose mother we buried today. I promised her the child would carry her name and the name of her father. I will raise the child and take good care to tell the little boy about his mother and as much as I know about his father. She has told me many tales of plans made by her father. Until her last breath she was distraught that she could not discover all of her father's secrets about a statue. It concerned her until her death. But I will do what I can to help the child to be a good person like his mother. This is my pledge that I write here in this book begun by Charlotte Beaufain Singleton and finished on this day December 11, 1865 by Amalie Holt.

The rest of the pages were blank.

"She died—Charlotte died after their baby boy was born." Tears stung Sarah's eyes. She gripped Jack's hand.

"Amalie Holt cared for Charlotte's and Jeremiah's child. And Holt! Jack, this diary was kept by Holt's family.

"His ancestor raised Jared Singleton," Jack said, and

flipped the pages carefully back to the front. Under Charlotte's name in small print, in the childish handwriting that belonged to Amalie Holt, was the name, Jared Singleton.

"Jared," he said. "That's a good name. Sounds strong and manly."

He looked at Sarah. She'd gone pale with a distant look in her eyes as if she was trying to figure out a very complicated math problem. She took the diary from him and carefully flipped through the pages. Between the last blank page, and the back cover of Charlotte's final diary was a photograph.

"Sarah? You okay?"

She turned slowly and looked at him. She said plainly and without emotion, as a statement of plain fact, "My great-grandfather's name was Jared Singleton."

She held the photo up so Jack could see it.

"I've seen this photo before. In my mother's cedar chest after she died."

Chapter 52

harleston Police Department headquarters was a whole lot busier than it had been yesterday when Sarah and Jack had been taken in for questioning. Today was just a formality. Statements they'd given yesterday were signed, a testament to the events of the last couple of days. Sarah related the events of the preceding evening and Jack gave a statement on what he'd seen at Rachel's house when he found her beaten in the garden. The police knew now he was nothing more than the person who found her. Rachel told them he'd been with her, trying to help and had gone only when the housekeeper arrived. They scolded him for leaving, but they were satisfied he wasn't a bad guy after all.

"How is Rachel?" Jack asked. He was worried despite all the hell she'd put them through and knowing now she'd found herself involved with dangerous people. In her own way she was trying to protect him and Sarah. He wouldn't want anything bad to happen to her.

"She's still in the hospital, but the doctors seem to think

she'll recover. It might take a while though. She was asking to see both of you," Skeet Mallory said.

Jack and Sarah turned to look at each other in the same instant. He knew Sarah would go with him to the hospital. They were a team now. And nothing Rachel could say or do would change that.

Chapter 53

Rachel's hospital room was filled with flowers from her family and sorority sisters with whom she maintained a social relationship. They'd been born into the same rarified strata and had settled in similar circles. Money seeks its own level, she used to tell Jack as they sipped expensive champagne over elegant dinners. But that was a lifetime ago.

Now she looked small and beaten. The bruises were the outward sign of what her eyes were saying—she was defeated. Things had not gone her way and it was time for retreat. He'd seen her like this once, in high school, when she'd gotten pregnant by one of the cadets at the Camden Military Academy and the cadet's family had whisked him back to Hyannis Port and left her with the consequences. She'd gone with one of her sorority sisters to New York—on a shopping trip, she told her parents. She begged Jack to go with her, but he'd been too horrified and too young to really grasp the nuances of the situation.

Besides he had the Junior Senior formal dance to attend. He was king of the ball and of course would never have abdicated his princely duties. Not back then anyway. He blushed at the recollection, not that he was the King of the prom, but that he'd ever been that shallow and that bad of a friend.

He sat next to Rachel's bed and took her hand. When her eyes fluttered open, he could see just how broken she was. A tear rolled down her cheek. Sarah stood just behind him, her hand on his shoulder. It was reassuring to have her there, to feel her hand on him.

"Rachel…" he said softly.

"Jack," she said, her voice thin and a little shaky. "I wanted to apologize to you and to Sarah for my abominable behavior the last few days. Can you ever forgive me?"

"Of course we can. You just need to get better so you can get back to your life."

"I'm going home to Camden. I need time to regroup," she said weakly.

"That's probably not a bad idea."

There was a moment of silence.

"How did you get involved with all of this?"

Rachel closed her eyes and winced.

"Holt was afraid. He felt Craig Duncan's murder was his fault." Jack and Sarah looked at each other.

"Holt had tracked Sarah down."

Sarah drew in an audible breath.

"Holt found the second diary among his mother's things when she died."

"Rachel…" Jack started to speak and Sarah squeezed his arm.

"Holt told me the second diary alluded to the hidden

treasure and of a map," her voice not much more than a whisper.

"And a letter. The diary mentioned a letter he believed held the final clues to the location of the statue head and its worth," Rachel coughed. "Water?"

Jack helped her with a glass of water and fitted the straw to her lips. She laid back down, took a shaky breath.

"Holt told Atkinson he was looking for a diary—that he believed it was hidden somewhere on campus with other items from the Civil War. He asked him if anything had been found during the renovation."

Her eyes grew large with the retelling and she grabbed Jack's arm.

"When Craig Duncan told Atkinson about the letter he'd found just a day after Sarah found the statue, Atkinson became obsessed with finding the treasure."

Rachel coughed, closed her eyes, her hand carefully fingering her bandaged neck.

"He thought the letter together with the diary answered all the questions. He was obsessed with it," she continued.

"Atkinson hired the blond man and promised him part of the treasure if he would get the letter for him."

"And blondie killed Craig for the letter?" Jack said, knowing the truth of it all.

"The man went rogue when he realized there was an enormous treasure. He followed Craig Duncan and eventually killed him for the letter. Holt found out about Atkinson and the blond," she said, and clutched Jack's hand tighter.

"Holt was terrified, felt it was his fault that evil had been unleashed. When he came to me and told me, I was so afraid you'd get hurt," she said. "I kicked you off the project to protect you both."

"How did Craig end up with the letter?" Sarah asked.

"Craig found the letter while doing research on architecture for the renovation. It was inside a book that belonged to someone named Singleton."

Rachel choked up. A tear rolled down her cheek.

In a few seconds she was able to continue.

"I had to stay involved with the inventory. It was obvious right away the real treasure was the head, and that it wasn't with the cache hidden behind the wall."

Sarah gripped Jack's hand as Rachel continued.

"When the hired gun—the big blond—came to my house, I didn't want to give him the diary you found. The one I took from your apartment, Sarah," her lip quivered, and she hesitated before continuing.

"I swear, I didn't hurt you though. The blond man followed me to your apartment and knocked you down trying to catch me."

"It's okay Rachel…" Sarah said, reaching out to touch her hand.

"The man—he beat me up—and he kicked me, then he took out a knife and…" Her hand went once more to her throat.

"I interrupted him," Jack whispered to no one, realizing how close Rachel had come to meeting the same fate as Craig Duncan.

Her voice rose with the excitement of the retelling of her ordeal. She was incredulous that someone would actually hit her and kick her, slit her throat.

"I didn't want to hurt you, Sarah. I was in a panic that either of you would get hurt. But…I also didn't want, didn't want you to know how stupid I'd been about everything."

Neither of them told her they had the head. They said

their goodbyes when the nurse came in to change the bandages on her neck.

Their next stop was to see an attorney, Jack's old friend Tucker Halsell.

Chapter 54

Tucker Wilkes Halsell III's offices were a vision of old world meets Charleston chic: thick colorful rugs over shining heart-pine wood floors, Tiffany-style lamps and heavily carved antiques shepherded over by efficient receptionists and assistants. Tucker was obviously doing okay.

They told him the whole story. When they got to the part about finding the statue head and discovering the gold and jewels inside, Tucker let out a little whistle that eased between the interesting gap in his front teeth.

"What we need to know is, to whom does the statue belong?" Jack asked.

"It belongs to the Beaufain family if you can find any direct heirs. I don't know of any that still live here, although there's still a street named for the family and there are a few buried in cemeteries around town." His Charleston drawl was completely charming as he leaned back in the worn leather swivel chair.

"Charlotte Beaufain was pregnant when she left town during the Civil War. That baby was named Jared Singleton—he was raised in Asheville by Charlotte's neighbor. Jared Singleton was Sarah's great-grandfather."

"Can you prove it?"

"Yes, I can. There is a photo of Jared Singleton found in the second diary," Sarah said, pulling the book from a tote bag full of items they deemed essential to this conversation. This photo is of the same person—in fact the same photo—as the one in my parent's house in Asheville. It should be simple to trace the family line."

Tucker leaned back in his chair. Sounds pretty simple. If it's true you're descended from Charlotte—and it sounds like her baby was the only child she had by Jeremiah—then your family would be heir to the goods. Do you have family?

"My father and my younger brothers. My mother died when I was a teenager."

"Then I guess it would go to your father."

Sarah's hands felt cold. Her father? Of course, he was the patriarch. And there was no doubt he needed the money.

"How do we tell the police what we found without losing control of it?"

"Technically at this point, all of it belongs to the college since that's where it was found. Once a provenance is established you can lay claim to it. There could be a lawsuit if the college decides to go that way…but my guess is they won't."

"They might want the treasure," Sarah said quietly.

"They might, and it could be deemed theirs, but I really don't think so. Is the statue itself valuable?"

"Without the head? Somewhat. Maybe a hundred thousand give or take ten. And the head is broken, so that hurts the value of course," Jack interjected.

Jack and Sarah looked at each other. They had a decision to make.

Chapter 55

Back at the apartment, Sarah called her father and questioned him about his parents and grandparents. If there was any doubt before, there was no doubt after the conversation. Her father had the family Bible that contained the names beginning with Charlotte and Jeremiah and ending with Sarah's youngest brother.

Why had she never connected the names? Or had she? Was that why she felt so drawn to Charlotte's diary? Did something in her memory trigger her reaction. Or had Charlotte reached out to her across time to finally complete the circle of her life? Had her grandmother's gift of knowing finally become her gift?

"Father, I have to tell you something. I found some things that belonged to Jared's mother, Charlotte. And now they belong to you."

"Lord, girl what are you talking about? Jared?"

Sarah explained about his great-grandfather Jared. She also shared the conversation she'd had with the lawyer. Her father was elated.

"How soon can I get that stuff?" he asked. "I sure could use the money as you are aware."

"Father, you are the likely owner, but it would be a really great thing for you to give them to the college," she said. "I would help you with the taxes.

"Well, now, that's a grand idea," he said, sounding jolly. Could he have changed that much? Was it possible he would donate the statue to the college for everyone to enjoy? Would he allow someone to care for the clothing and the diaries?

"Very grand indeed. But I'm a poor farmer and don't intend to give away the only inheritance I'll ever get, even if it does come a few generations late. So how soon do you think it will be 'til you can get the stuff to me?"

"Soon, Father, soon," she said, dispirited, sad they would never see things the same way; sad his life was so devoid of meaning. Just sad about the outcome of this great adventure of discovery about her own past.

"Sounds like that statue might pay for me to retire. I guess I was wrong about you, girl. You are good for something."

"I'm glad for you, Father," she said before ending the conversation.

She said nothing through dinner. Jack didn't ask her about the conversation. She didn't want to tell him her father intended sell the head and all the rest. Jack scrambled some eggs for them and made toast from the baguette from yesterday.

She was sad her father didn't understand the worth of the items beyond the money they would bring. That the statue would be gone forever was almost more than she could contemplate.

That night as they lay in bed, Jack held her, but the fire had disappeared from her soul. She had an ache that seemed impossible to resolve. She left the bed in the middle of the night to sit on the widow's walk. Even in the dark of the night, container ships cruised in and out of the harbor. She would have to leave this place. She would have to find her home somewhere else. To stay would remind her of Charlotte and Jeremiah, and her great-grandfather Jared. To stay she would have to admit she was embarrassed by her father's plan.

To stay would mean she'd have to deal with loving Jack Chase. To stay would require a lot of work. Leaving would be clean and simple. Starting over anywhere in the world she wanted to go would be distracting. It would be new. It would be easy. She would have a life similar to the one she'd found here and enjoyed before it became complicated.

She remembered sitting up here in the afternoon a few days earlier. Her introspection had revealed a life of observation in place of participation. Well, she'd certainly been a participant this week, and it was unsettling. It was draining and at times downright frightening. But she'd not been a spectator.

She went back downstairs and crawled into her bed and snuggled next to Jack, in part because he was pretty much sprawled all over it, and in part, because she wanted to be close to him tonight.

A decision was on the horizon and her choices were agonizing. She was afraid of what she would choose.

Chapter 56

When Sarah woke, Jack was gone. Good. She had things to think about—lots of things. And she wanted time alone to sort through what she needed for the next part of her life.

She was an average working person with a very uncaring, unthinking father as a parent. Her mother had died in sadness. Her brothers followed in their father's footsteps.

Who was she like? She felt a kinship with Jeremiah and with Charlotte. Her great-great-grandparents. Would she have felt at home with them?

She slipped into the shower and washed her hair, lathered her body and felt the heat of the water as she agonized toward her decision.

Jack. How could she feel this way, when she knew already what her decision had to be? It was simply too hard to believe they could have a future together. Once the thrill of this chase was over—which, in essence, it already was—then he would be off to resume his life as part of the international arts scene.

Already he was being courted. Already, she could see the gleam in his eye at the possibilities that had opened to him since the news of the statue had hit.

Granted, she'd received a fair amount of attention, too. She'd had several substantial offers from other schools, and one from a prominent auction house in New York. She was flattered, but a little afraid to imagine herself in a big-city arena.

But what about Jack? It was fun now but wouldn't it be better to end it herself? Better than to risk giving herself to him completely only to watch him disappear? Better to take the pain that was sure to come in her own hands?

The decision was hers and hers alone.

Be brave.

The words played in the back of her mind. She thought of her ancestors, their bravery. Their lives were cut short. What would they have given for the opportunity she and Jack had only to seize?

When the knock came at her door, she wrapped her wet hair in a towel and opened to the smiling face of Jack Chase.

"Hi," he said.

"Hi."

"You need to come with me. I have something to show you."

"Do I have to?" she stood, a hand on one hip, a smile on her face.

"Yes. You have to. It's important," he said. "Now get dressed."

"Important? Okay then. Why didn't you say so to start with?" Within the hour they were speeding down King Street toward the college.

"Where're we going?"

"The college gallery."

"Jack! No! It's too painful. I can't," she called to him over the traffic sounds.

"You're tough. You can take it," he said as he expertly maneuvered her car into a tight spot.

Chapter 57

It seemed like forever since he'd first come into the gallery but it'd only been a couple of weeks. He had a memory glimpse of Sarah standing in front of the statue, her hands exploring its torso that first day when he arrived in Charleston.

"Jack," she said as he closed the door to the outside world. "This is so very, very hard for me. Please. Don't make me look at the statue."

He stood in front of her, put his hands on her shoulders, and said straight into her face.

"You are the bravest woman I've ever met. And the smartest. And if this weren't important, I wouldn't ask you to be here. Okay?"

"Okay," she said quietly. He watched her gather courage to face the statue she knew her father had already sold to an anonymous collector. It made her physically ill to even think about it.

Jack opened the door to the main gallery and glanced

inside, his heart racing with anticipation as she stepped through the opening into the gallery. A lone light shone down on the spot where the statue stood—the whole statue.

Her face opened in surprise. She turned to look at him, then back to the statue.

She cautiously walked forward. Jack cleared his throat to get her attention as he held out to her the latex gloves.

"I think you'll be needing these," he said. She slipped them on and traced her finger down the leg, then reached up to the face of the statue.

He knew he'd done the right thing.

"Jack? How?"

"I wanted you to see it whole. It needs more work, but for now, this was the best I could do." He was surprised at how well the restorer had done on such a short time. The head was positioned exactly as it should be with the mend barely noticeable. The statue was spectacular.

"Thank you. Thank you so much for letting me see it like this," she said, smiling broadly, walking around the statue several times, admiring the whole piece for the first time.

"It's yours," Jack said.

"For a while at least. My father has a buyer and has already reached an agreement to sell it all. He'll get a lot less than it's really worth, but the cash means more to him than haggling it out piece by piece."

"Yes. I know. I bought it. It's yours."

"But, my father...."

"On loan to the school for as long as you want it to be. But you are the owner."

"I don't understand."

"I bought it from him. And I'm giving it to you. It's yours."

She didn't speak for a few beats before saying, "Jack. I can't."

"It's already done," he handed her the bill of sale from her father. It showed her as the owner. He also had an insurance policy that listed her as the owner.

"Jack. This is too much. I can't accept this."

"This belongs to you. And there's a clause in there that says as soon as possible you should sell some of the jewels to repay me—and if you ever sell the statue, you have to give me half the money." He laughed because he knew she'd never sell it. "This head is the marble shell that held the gold and jewels, Sarah. The gold head itself is in pieces. It really can't be mended. Even if it could be, the college has told me they don't want the liability of having to secure it. It would cost them a fortune—not to mention all the sleepless nights. I've asked a jewel appraiser to give you a net worth on the jewels and the gold. They can be sold in whole or in part..."

"Jack... they are yours now, not mine."

"Ms. Singleton," a voice called from the far end of the gallery. A man emerged from the dark corner. She recognized him as a member of the board, Dr. Tindal.

"On behalf of the college, I would like to thank you for your decision to let the college display your statue for the next year. It is most generous. And thank your father for me for donating the household goods and the diary to the college. A generous donation."

"He donated the..." she realized he would not have donated the items had they been worth anything much."

"The college recognizes your contribution to this project and would like very much to make you an offer."

"An offer of what kind, Dr. Tindal?"

"Without you, it is very likely this entire group of artifacts would have been stolen or destroyed. You have an instinct for this kind of work. Your supervisor, Rachel Stover, has recommended you as the curator for the exhibit and suggests we snap you up as her replacement as our director of acquisitions before someone else does."

"I don't know what to say." Sarah's delight was impossible to hide. And Jack was surprised and delighted the college was finally recognizing the contribution Sarah made in bringing the project to a happy conclusion.

"Well, we understand your great-great grandfather was a professor here—and an author. I believe he was also a patriot who gave his life in battle. You are part of this college, Ms. Singleton, and we are very eager to have you on our staff. This project has already brought us a great deal of recognition. Donations to sustain and expand the collection have already started coming in. We hope you will say yes. We understand you may need some time to think it over."

Chapter 58

arah looked at Jack, Dr. Tindal and the statue.

Again she walked toward the marble man, surveyed it, and smiled. It was hers to do with as she wished. And at the same time, she could pay Jack back. Was it just possible dreams could come true?

She walked to Jack and stood tall before him.

The decision she'd made at the apartment, to be brave and to follow her heart, was right. She could see on his face his concern she would reject him. She held her arms out to him and he immediately embraced her.

She ran her fingers through the curl of his hair as it lay against his neck, curiously feeling the thin chain that held his medallion.

And when he whispered, "You're an incredible woman, Sarah," she pulled away and looked up at him. She could see the emotion building in his eyes and recognized the same feelings growing in her heart.

"And you, Jack Chase, are one very interesting man. I just might have to spend more time figuring you out."

And when their lips met, everything she really needed to know was in that one kiss.

Acknowledgments

In the beginning and always, a special thank you goes to my family – Pat, Sean and Maya, Paul and Kim – who are all supportive, long-suffering and willing to let me share their lives with faithful readers. And a special thank you to the grandgirl Rook and grandboy Kallan for putting a perpetual smile on my face.

And to all those who have supported my writing over the years: Barbara Hill and the Summerville Writers Guild; my magical critique partners of whom I am always in awe: Nina Bruhns, Vicki Wilkerson, Dorothy McFalls; lifelong friend Mary Ann Blaskowitz and who read the first draft of this novel even after a pelican pooped on it one afternoon at Holden Beach. She also offered her eagle eye to the book cover; Frank Johnson who is a constant source of encouragement; my sister Jeannie for doing a final read through of The Diary; my sister Janice and her husband Jim for always taking time to listen; my parents, the late Jack and Nelle Stein; and a host of aunts, uncles and cousins;

And all of the friends and readers who have been there for me more years than I can count.

With love and gratitude always,
J.S. Watts
January 25, 2015
N. Charleston, S.C.

About the Author

Judy Watts is an award-winning writer and photographer. Her first three books are collections of her more than 900 columns published in newspapers throughout the Lowcountry.

Watts' new writing project, the Charleston Chase Mystery series, is written under the name J. Sinclair Watts, to honor her grandmother, Kate Sinclair.

Living with Wieners and Guys, too; Living with Manchildren; Living with The Hubster; and the Charleston Chase Mystery series' first offering *The Diary*, are all available on Amazon or at judywattsauthor.